THE SECOND SEDUCTION
OF A LADY

Also by Miranda Neville

Confessions from an Arranged Marriage
The Amorous Education of Celia Seaton
The Dangerous Viscount
The Wild Marquis
Never Resist Temptation

THE SECOND SEDUCTION OF A LADY

MIRANDA NEVILLE

AVONIMPULSE

An Imprint of HarperCollinsPublishers

Excerpt from *The Importance of Being Wicked* copyright © 2012 by Miranda Neville.

Excerpt from *The Forbidden Lady* copyright © 2002, 2012 by Kerrelyn Sparks.

Excerpt from *Turn to Darkness* copyright © 2012 by Tina Wainscott.

EPub Edition NOVEMBER 2012 ISBN: 9780062243362

Print Edition ISBN: 9780062243379

10 9 8 7 6 5 4

THE SECOND SEDUCTION
OF A LADY

CHAPTER ONE

Somerset, England, 1793

If not for that one time, that evening of insanity following a week of madness, Eleanor Hardwick would hold an unblemished record for common sense. Luckily no one knew the full extent of her folly. No one except *him*.

The memory of the two weeks that followed still caused her stomach to drop. The waiting, the fear, until the onset of the dull throb that signaled her liberation from the possible consequences of her indiscretion. Many a foolish female must have felt the same way. But while most were relieved not to be with child because they faced nothing but unwed disgrace, Eleanor was happy because it saved her from the necessity of matrimony. She had fetched her women's cloths, packed half a dozen unopened letters into a neat parcel, and sent the missives back to their sender with a brief, stinging request to contact her no more.

Eleanor believed in common sense with a fervor that bordered on the dogmatic. She did not believe in marriage, a conclusion arrived at through the dispassionate observation of her many friends and relations. Who could possibly admire an institution that allowed a malodorous toad like Sir George Ashdown to impregnate her cousin Sylvia six times in seven years? Or bound together a pair with as little in common as her own parents?

When, at the age of twenty-one, she gained control of an income of five hundred pounds a year from her late mother, she resolved to spend her life in an entirely rational fashion. And if reason led her to lavish a large proportion of that income on personal adornment, who was to argue with her? No husband would ever carp at her milliner's bills.

For almost a decade she had divided her time between her father's house and traveling for prolonged visits to those of her relations, their spouses, and offspring. Thus she gained all the enjoyment of domesticity without its undesirable permanent effects. Though not without her share of suitors, she had discouraged them all without regret.

Except one.

The sole occasion she allowed her heart to override her reason had *not* been a success. In fact, she rarely allowed herself to remember it, except on those occasions when she awoke in a state of melancholy, clutching her midriff. She ascribed this foolishness to overindulgence in cheese.

As a result of her rapport with the younger generation, she was much in demand when impetuous youth fell into undesirable company, or in love with unsuitable men. On the whole she found erring children easier to deal with than their frantic parents, confirming her conclusion that marriage did strange things to the adult mind.

In the case of her father's second cousin, the Honorable Mrs. George Brotherton, it was two marriages. But Eleanor doubted matrimony was responsible for her condition. Such a combination of malice and stupidity must surely be innate. And her two husbands, discovering that the only escape from marriage was death, had chosen that drastic course. Only a certain physical likeness convinced Eleanor that young Caro Brotherton wasn't a changeling. How a chilly beauty like Elizabeth Brotherton had managed to conceive such a delightful creature was beyond understanding.

"I despair of Caroline," Mrs. Brotherton said over teacups, the day after Eleanor arrived in Somerset in response to an urgent summons. "Look at her! She is a disgrace."

Eleanor looked. Caro's red curls were a little untidy, and down around her shoulders. Perfectly acceptable for a seventeen-year-old who wasn't yet out. One foot bounced against the leg of her chair, but her hands were busy with an embroidery hoop.

"What are you making, Caro?" Eleanor asked, hoping to draw attention to this ladylike pursuit.

"A pair of slippers for Uncle Camber."

Eleanor had stepped in a wasps' nest. Though Mrs. Brotherton had always loved a lord, the Earl of Camber loathed his widowed sister-in-law and never invited her to his estate when Caro made her annual visit. If not for her own fondness for the child, Eleanor would never seek out Elizabeth's company either.

"I shouldn't let you go to Camber," Mrs. Brotherton said with a sniff. "He's a bad influence."

"I thought he was virtually bedridden," Eleanor said, to forestall the furious response on the tip of Caro's tongue.

"Poor Uncle Camber," Caro said, obviously struggling for

serenity. "His feet get cold." Then, after an uneasy silence, "Lucy Markham is going to Bath in September to stay with her aunt. She says I can go with her. You must let me go, Mama."

Caro had never learned how to approach her mother with tact. "Certainly not!" was the predictable reply. "You will wait until next season when you will make your debut under my eye."

"It's so unfair! You don't want me to have any fun."

"Cousin," Eleanor said, leaping into her role as peacemaker. "I need some fresh air. If you aren't too tired, Caro, I'd enjoy your company."

Caro accepted the escape and the aspersion on her vigor with all the energy of her years. "Yes please, dearest Eleanor! You're such a nice, fast walker!"

"Fetch your bonnet!" Eleanor spoke too late. Caro had already bolted the room.

"I'm so glad you are here," Caro said, once they had escaped the dreary atmosphere of Sedgehill Manor into the lane. "At least with you I may call on our neighbors. Mama doesn't think any of them are good enough for her. I wish my papa had not been the brother of an earl."

"Cousin Elizabeth does tend to be just the slightest bit high in the instep." An outrageous understatement about a woman who would probably address Queen Charlotte herself with condescension. She was well aware that Elizabeth tolerated her only because Eleanor's father, although a country parson, was nephew to a viscount.

"It's so unfair!" The eternal complaint of youth and one that in this case Eleanor found justified.

"I have an idea," she said. "I'm going to London for a month in the autumn. Shall I ask your mother if you can accompany me?"

"Darling, darling Eleanor." Caro positively bounced with glee. "That would be wonderful." Then her face fell. "Mama will never say yes."

"I will try to persuade her. As you may have guessed, she invited me here because she thinks I'm a sensible influence. Let's prove her right. You must be *very* good."

"I hate being good! And it won't work. Nothing I do is ever enough for her. She won't let me go. She wants to force me to marry a horrid old man."

"Surely not."

"She does, I tell you. She's picked out a marquess."

"How old is this man?"

"At least thirty!" Caro cried tragically.

"At death's door!" replied Eleanor, who had herself reached that dread age at her last birthday. "Perhaps, if you are very lucky, you'll meet a suitable gentleman who is a year or two younger."

"Don't tease, Eleanor. I will marry only when I fall in love, and I could never fall in love with such a dull creature."

In Eleanor's experience, girls got such ideas from only one source. "Have you been reading novels? I'm surprised Cousin Elizabeth allows it."

"She doesn't. Mama wants me to read only improving books. I borrow them from Lucy. I just finished *The Battlements of Adelmante*. Orlando, the most delicious and dashing man, saves Loriana from being drowned in the moat by a ghost."

"Drowned by a ghost? Fancy that! I must read this remarkable book."

"And then they fall desperately in love," she said, peeping sideways at Eleanor, "but their love is *doomed* because Loriana's cruel guardian wishes her to marry a wicked count!" She gave a blissful sigh, though that was a feeble word to describe an expression that seemed to possess every inch of her slight, muslin-clad body. "I can't wait to fall in love. Have you ever been in love, Eleanor?"

"Never." Eleanor wasn't really lying. She'd only *thought* she was in love for a few days. Once she discovered the truth about Max Quinton, any tender sentiment had vanished from her breast, evaporated into air as though it never existed. Such an insubstantial emotion could not possibly have been true love. "Love is not for me," she said. "I'm far too sensible."

Caro accepted the denial with an incredulous shrug. At seventeen, she wasn't much interested in the affairs of others, especially those as ancient as Eleanor. "I shall never marry without love, not even if Mama locks me in the dungeon."

"Does Sedgehill Manor have a dungeon? Quite unusual for a house not more than fifty years old."

"You know what I mean. You are so lucky not to have a mother telling you what to do."

"As to that, my dear, I do miss my mine, who died when I was even younger than you are." Because Eleanor believed in encouraging good conduct, even under the most trying of circumstances, she added, "And you would miss yours."

Caro seized her hand. "I'm sorry, Eleanor. I shouldn't have said that about your mama."

"It's all right. And you are right. I am fortunate to have my own funds and a father so wrapped in his studies he lets me do as I wish. But only," she continued, seeing a moment for a lesson while she had Caro's volatile attention, "because I am sensible and he knows I won't get into trouble."

"You've never done anything foolish in all these years?"

"Never." Unless one counted losing one's virtue to a rogue.

"I don't know how you manage it."

Eleanor tried to keep from smiling and to instill some common sense into the girl, with advice on the management of implacable parents. She couldn't flatter herself Caro paid much attention. About a mile from the house, they turned off the lane, climbing a stile into a water meadow. The lazy river glimmered invitingly in the sun, a fisherman forming a picturesque vista on the opposite bank.

Caro ran to the water's edge and stared. Since her straw bonnet had long since slipped off and trailed down her back, she raised a hand to her brow to ward off the high sun. Eleanor, generally averse to hyperbole, had to admit the angler resembled a young Apollo: slender and lithe, with golden hair ruffled by the breeze. Most improperly dressed, with nothing but an open-necked shirt above his breeches, he flung aside his fishing rod and favored Caro with a dazzling smile.

"Why dost thou shade thy lovely face? Oh why," he quoted Francis Quarles, stretching out his arms in a manner worth of Drury Lane.

> "Does that eclipsing hand so long deny
> The sunshine of thy soul-enliv'ning eye?"

Caro's literary borrowings hadn't included much poetry. "Did you just make that up?" she called across a dozen feet of water.

"You would inspire me to original verse, except your beauty has addled my senses."

Eleanor surged forward. This kind of nonsense would turn a young girl's head and bring down the wrath of Cousin Elizabeth. "Caro, remember your manners. You are not acquainted with this gentleman."

For a gentleman he was. That, at least, Eleanor could tell from his voice and demeanor. She tried to recall if she'd met the owners of this land on previous visits to Somerset. Townley or Townsend was their name.

"Allow me to introduce myself and make my bow to you ladies."

"You're on the wrong side of the river!" Caro objected.

"Easily remedied," he said, and slid down into the water, boots and all.

Caro let out a peal of laughter and stepped nearer to the bank. Being Caro, she tumbled in. The golden youth waded into the center of the stream, where the water was waist high, and gathered her into his arms. With some difficulty—carrying a wet, full-grown girl would be hard for a far larger man—he staggered to the bank, where the pair of them gazed into each other's eyes for a long moment.

"Caro!" Eleanor called. The idiot boy had borne her back to his side of the river. "What a foolish thing to do. You're wet through."

Caro ignored her. "You saved my life!" she said dramatically.

"I would circle the earth three times to do so again and fight a thousand Mamluks for the privilege of bearing such a precious burden."

Seeing that the precious burden was testing his strength, and he was in danger of dropping her back in the river, Eleanor coughed loudly. The besotted pair looked up in surprise. "I think you should put her down, sir."

With surprising agility, he let the precious burden to the ground. Wet, clinging muslin revealed every contour of Caro's enviable figure, a sight that her savior regarded with appreciation. Hair and water streamed over her shoulders as her bonnet floated downstream.

"Caro!" Eleanor's cry was ignored. The pair had recommenced their mutual gazing. She eyed the water, but had no intention of getting wet and ruining her blue cambric gown. "Hey! Young sir! Is there a bridge close by?"

No answer. The youth was holding Caro's hand. If Eleanor didn't intervene soon he'd be kissing her and she didn't trust the girl to resist the liberty. Quite the opposite. A little downstream, beyond a curve, she glimpsed a crossing. A few planks of wood hardly merited the title of bridge, but it would do.

Max Quinton took his angling seriously. That's why he'd elected to occupy a spot a couple of hundred yards away from Robert, who tended to lose concentration. While Max found his ward's aesthetical theories and literary jests entertaining enough, they scared away the fish. When he heard talking, splashing, and shrieking upstream, he had a trout on the line, a stubborn one that required all his skill and enough agility to make him glad the warmth of the day had made him discard his riding coat. The curve of the stream and a thicket obstructed his view. Deciding Robert could handle any crisis—the river was neither fast nor deep enough to easily drown in—he continued to play his fish. Intent on what was happening underwater, at first he barely registered a woman striding by on the opposite bank. It took a moment or two for his consciousness to note a resemblance to her. To Eleanor.

Every so often he'd catch a glimpse of a tall, trim figure in a crowd and his heart would leap. But it never was her. The world, it sometimes seemed, was full of well-dressed brunettes. He hadn't set eyes on Eleanor Hardwick in almost five years. In a crowded street or an assembly, it wasn't unreasonable to anticipate an encounter. Any such expectation in a Somerset meadow, many miles from either of their homes, was irrational. Still, as always, he had to be sure. Blue cloth flashed among the branches of a willow. His inattention allowed the line to slacken; his trout broke away from the hook. It had been a large one.

One that got away. Just like Eleanor.

The woman, who was not, of course, Eleanor, passed out of sight. Forgetting his state of undress, Max wedged his rod into a bush, headed downstream and rounded the thicket that concealed the simple bridge. The woman set foot on the narrow boards of the crossing. His lungs emptied.

Her grace was the first thing he'd noticed about her at the Petworth assembly, a human equivalent of the thoroughbred horses he bred. No, not human. She was a goddess come to earth. High breasts, a trim waist, and curved hips. And long shapely legs. Even though covered by a gown, he'd known, the minute he set eyes on her, that her legs would be something special. And then there was her face. She would never be called pretty. There was too much strength in her features, the proud brow and nose, the cool, amused gaze that surveyed the world about her and found it full of fools that required her tolerance.

He hadn't forgotten a single moment of his brief acquaintance with Eleanor Hardwick, and for five years, not a day had passed when he failed to regret its loss. While he acknowledged his own wrongdoing in his courtship and seduction, the end had been her decision. Anger had fought regret and sometimes prevailed. He'd wondered about his reaction when they met again. Now he knew.

"Eleanor!" She looked up. He stepped forward to meet her on the bridge. "Eleanor!" He should ask her how she was, why she was there. But he didn't care why she was there. All he wanted to do was take her into his arms and tease her stern mouth into returning his kisses.

His outstretched arms were welcomed with a hearty shove and he landed on his back in cold water.

"What—"

She looked down at him, grim satisfaction on her elegant features. "I beg your pardon, Mr. Quinton, but you were in my way. I have things to attend to."

As he struggled upright in the thigh-deep water, she completed her crossing. Cold soaked through every garment, chilling his skin, his ardor, and his heart. "Wait! You are trespassing," he called, a surge of rage making him petty.

He'd been wrong, yes, but his intentions had ultimately been honorable. She had sent him about his business with a cold rebuke. And returned all his letters unread.

"Oh? Is this your land?" she said, arching a haughty brow, knowing well that his home was over a hundred miles away, near Newmarket.

"Effectively, yes," he said, clambering up the bank. "I have control of the Townsend estate for another three weeks, until my ward reaches his majority."

"In that case," she replied, "I'll collect *my* charge and be off."

Ignoring the squelching in his boots, he reached for her again. In the bare second his wet hand rested on her lower arm, warm under his chilled fingers, longing flooded his veins. "Eleanor," he whispered.

"Get your wet hands off my gown." She shook him off.

"Won't you forgive me?"

Her gray eyes held his. He'd seen them bright with affection and wild with ecstasy. Now they contained polished steel.

"I think, Mr. Quinton, it would be better if we both forget that there is anything to forgive."

Max deliberately mistook her meaning. "Good," he said. She watched with the outrage of a dowager as he unbuttoned his clammy, clinging waistcoat. Yet she'd seen him wearing even less. Or felt him, rather. It had been dark at the time.

The garment slid down his arms. "I'm ready to apologize again, but I'd like it even better if we could begin a new chapter. May we start again? Please Eleanor."

Eleanor watched Max Quinton drape his wet waistcoat over a branch, in fascinated disbelief that, meeting him after five years, he should be stripping off his clothes. She trusted he wouldn't be removing all of them. The entreaty in his voice affected her, but only for an instant. Giving him a dunking had blunted the edge of anger that his appearance provoked, that was all. Nothing else had changed.

"I made it clear in the past," she said, "that our acquaintance was over. Forever. Should we meet again, which I trust won't be necessary, you may call me Miss Hardwick."

"Don't you think that's absurd, given what we once were to each other?"

She stepped farther away from this unpleasantly damp man. Never mind that his figure was displayed to advantage beneath clinging linen, fine enough to limn the contours of his chest and reveal an intriguing dark shadow descending to the waist. It was true that his thick, wavy hair looked quite good wet, but she no longer responded to the lilt of laughter in his deep voice. "Our past relationship was founded on falsehood and meant nothing. I never think of you and I'd like to keep it that way. We meet as indifferent strangers."

A smile tugged on his lips. It was one of the first things she'd noticed about him, that hint of humor in an otherwise grave face. "Do you often push strangers into rivers?"

"You deserved it."

"I'll own up to my transgressions and again humbly beg for your forgiveness. I have never held you in anything but the greatest esteem." He sounded reasonable and earnest. The sincerity in his voice plucked at her heart.

She'd be a fool, again, to believe him. "I was nothing but a game to you, a conquest to impress your friends."

"You were my love, the woman I wanted to marry."

She answered in precise, clipped syllables. "You *wanted* to marry me because you had no choice. I appreciated the honor you did me with your forced proposal, but declined to tie myself for life to such a man, for such a reason."

She would have stalked off, but he stayed her with a hand on her elbow. "You insult me, Eleanor, and you are wrong," he said. "It's true that I owed you marriage but I didn't offer for you solely because I had to. You were not compromised, not publicly, as is proven by the fact that your reputation is intact."

Again she shook him off. "No thanks to you! I was the subject of a drunken wager. Do you deny it?"

"I cannot, to my shame, though it was not I who made the bet. It was Ashdown. I wanted no part of it until I set eyes on you."

Far from placated, she spun around to confront him. "Am I supposed to be flattered by that?" she demanded, putting her hands on her hips and glaring at him. "Is it acceptable that you took part in a contest for my favors because you discovered that I wasn't quite the dried-up spinster Sir George Ashdown had claimed?"

"That is not how it was." His voice had lost its soothing tone and she was glad of it. It was only fair that he should be as agitated as she.

"But you took the money. You won the competition and collected your winnings. Will you deny it?"

"You are willfully misunderstanding me. I'd have kissed you even if there wasn't a penny in it for me."

Kiss! He'd done a great deal more than kiss! "I really don't care," she said with her nose in the air. "I was overcome by the proximity of a charming rogue on a summer night, not the first foolish woman to make such a mistake and doubtless not the last. Luckily no lasting harm was done."

Voices intruded, Robert's and a young female's. Max looked around as they came into view. From the state of their garments, it appeared both had suffered the same fate as he. The three of them were dripping wet, while Eleanor stood immaculate and dry, her clothing as unruffled as her heart. She could very well be the officious harridan who had been described to him before he set eyes on her.

It had been at a dinner hosted by the Earl of Egremont for the officers of the Sussex militia.

"You want to hear about pestilential females?" The question came from Sir George Ashdown, one of the local gentry summoned to Petworth Park for this all-male occasion. "There's no woman who's more of a nuisance than my wife's cousin Eleanor."

There were some embarrassed protests from the officers. The topic of conversation had been women and the traps they set for unwitting men. Women, not ladies. It really wasn't proper for a group of gentlemen, who'd left the dinner table to take the air, to discuss *ladies*.

"Damn it, Ashdown." The speaker was the major of the regiment who had invited Max down to Sussex for the week-long race meeting. "I wouldn't discuss any cousin of mine when my cock's pissing in the wind." The earl's claret had been good and plentiful and the major's words were slurred.

So were Ashdown's. "Button it up then. Complain all you want about your birds of paradise, but at least you can be rid of them. There's no disposing of a wife."

"You're talking about Lady Ashdown?" Another officer was confused as well as disapproving.

"Lady Ashdown never gave me any trouble until Eleanor Hardwick came to stay with us. Now it's nothing but nagging, all day long. No muddy boots in the house, no wet dogs in the drawing room, and she won't let me bed her when I'm drunk." Sir George arranged his breeches. "The haughty bitch Eleanor put her up to it."

Max did not regard himself a fastidious man. He bred horses and spent much of his life in the stables. But he was inclined to be on the side of Ashdown's wife in this matter. Though no judge of male allure, he had the feeling that if he was Lady Ashdown, he'd try to avoid bedding Sir George, who possessed a large belly and an unpleasant odor, at every opportunity.

"You know what?" Ashdown continued, aggrieved. "She asked me to bathe more often. I bathe! Once a month. Just like my father. Always have, always will."

Some of the officers, the married men among them, made sympathetic noises and a couple of them mentioned interfering female relations.

"Interfering is right. She has no business telling my wife what to do. She's a cold-hearted bitch and could never get a man of her own. Who would want her? Needs to be put in her place."

A despicable man, Ashdown, still was. He had been flat wrong about Eleanor. But that crude complaint of Sir George's had eventually led to the destruction of Max's hopes.

An insistent female voice brought him back to Somerset, where he had improbably encountered his lost love.

"Eleanor!" cried the girl. "This is Robert Townsend, our

neighbor. Imagine! We met when we were little children but he hasn't lived here in years. Now he has returned for his twenty-first birthday, and his guardian is to celebrate it with a grand ball!"

Eleanor's presence was explained. She must be visiting relations in the neighborhood. She had a great many relations.

"Robert," he said. "I see you've managed to get into trouble, as usual. I believe introductions are in order. I am already acquainted with Miss Hardwick."

Robert knew how to behave when he wanted to. Despite his wet clothes he produced a bow and his most winning smile. "Delighted to make your acquaintance, ma'am."

Eleanor curtsied. "You met my cousin in midstream, and I daresay you introduced yourselves. But now we are on dry land, let's try for a little formality. Mr. Townsend, allow me to present Miss Caroline Brotherton." Five years ago, he'd been charmed by her quips. Time had not changed that at all.

The girl, a pretty creature with a mop of damp red hair, shivering in an indecently clinging gown, curtsied without taking her eyes off Robert. Max coughed.

Eleanor's voice turned from amused raillery back to frost. "Caro. This is Mr. Quinton. I believe he is Mr. Townsend's guardian."

"Only for three more weeks! How do you and Max know each other, Miss Hardwick?"

Max waited with interest to hear her answer.

"We met in Sussex several years ago. Our acquaintance was of the slightest."

That was one way of putting it. Measured in time their acquaintance had, indeed, been slight.

CHAPTER TWO

Eleanor had hoped never to see Max Quinton again. But if she had to, there was a certain satisfaction in having pushed him into the river. Then he had the nerve to beg her pardon. The gall of the man! And he had the nerve to look extremely fine, even when dripping wet. And, unlike her, he had the presence of mind to fetch his dry coat for Caro, not the first time he'd demonstrated such chivalry. In the cool of a summer night, he'd draped his evening coat around Eleanor's shoulders as they'd sat beside a Sussex lake.

Hurrying Caro home before she caught a cold, Eleanor continued to dwell on the way Max's clothes clung to his well-developed sportsman's physique. Unlike his friend Sir George Ashdown, loathsome husband to Cousin Sylvia, he'd kept his figure despite being past his first youth. Pretty good for nearly forty.

Who was she fooling? She knew quite well that he was thirty-five and a half, exactly five years older than she. Their birthdays were two days apart. It was absurd the way trivial facts lingered in the memory, facts as unimportant as what she had for dinner on Tuesday. Except that she couldn't remember last week's menu and she was annoyingly aware of Max Quinton's preference for lamb over beef, for apple tart over syllabub. He preferred Shakespeare to the modern poets, the country to the town.

She had first seen him at the Petworth Inn, at an assembly initiating the week of the militia races. The cluster of officers who'd surrounded her, begging to stand up with her, had been a surprise. Though no wallflower, she'd never been a beauty, and at twenty-five she approached spinster or chaperone status. She put her sudden popularity down to the shortage of younger ladies owing to the sudden influx of officers at the humble provincial assembly. Nevertheless, she had enjoyed the unexpected attention. A sea of red coats and eager faces pressed around her. She'd been laughing, attempting to distribute her dances among the supplicants, when she noticed him.

A tall, broad-shouldered man, visible over the crowd, he'd stood a little apart, his evening dress marking him a civilian. With his craggy features and prominent nose, he wasn't handsome by most standards. Lightly tanned skin spoke of a life lived outdoors. Locks of brown hair fell over a broad forehead and raked the collar of his coat. He'd regarded the proceedings with a careless expression. Perhaps it was the sobriety of his dress, but he struck her as a sensible man, in contrast to the soldiers strutting in their uniforms and swords.

Then she'd happened to catch his gaze. They looked at each other and his indifference turned to warmth. In the weathered face his eyes stood out very blue, as did white teeth revealed by a dawning smile. Her heart seemed to stop . . .

"I'm in love!"

Caro's exclamation brought her back to the present.

"It's true," the girl insisted. "Who ever loved who loved not at first sight?" Caro's ignorance of poetry didn't extend to *Romeo and Juliet*. "No sooner did I lay eyes on Robert than I knew. I shall love him forever."

"Nonsense!" Eleanor said. She was in a position to know.

"I shall! You don't understand, Eleanor!"

Eleanor also knew better than to argue with an infatuated girl. "He seems very pleasant," she said. "How delightful for you to meet an old playmate after all this time."

Her attempt at painting Townsend as a callow youth failed to impress. From the vantage point of seventeen, Caro saw the twenty-year-old as the perfect romantic figure. And so she should. For a first flirtation, Robert Townsend was quite suitable, and as long as she kept an eye on her little cousin, it would be nothing more. While she realized that not every woman preferred spinsterhood, she thought disaster even more assured when marriage was entered too young. Sylvia had been seventeen when she wed Ashdown. Eleanor's own mother had wed at the same age.

Caro chattered at her side. "Robert has been to Italy and France and Holland, you know? He writes poetry and knows all about art. Isn't Robert the most beautiful name? Do you think Mama will let him call on us? I shall die if I never see him again. Die!"

"Since Mr. Townsend is visiting his estate, I expect we'll meet him in the neighborhood," Eleanor replied cheerfully. More cheerfully than she felt. Meeting Mr. Townsend also meant meeting his guardian.

"**R**obert Townsend is back," John Mathews stated the next morning. Elizabeth Brotherton's son by her first marriage, John resembled his mother in character if not looks. His simplest remarks were always delivered with the weight of momentous opinions. "We won't wish to pursue the acquaintance."

Eleanor quelled Caro's rising protest with a frown. She'd helped the girl creep into the house and change into dry clothes without being discovered. Somehow Caro had managed to keep silent for almost an entire day, but Eleanor wouldn't wager a farthing on her continued discretion if she didn't soon get a chance to meet her youthful neighbor.

"Why not?" Mrs. Brotherton asked. "I haven't seen him since he was a boy, but we visited his late parents. Both your father and Mr. Brotherton approved of them."

"I don't like to gossip," John said mendaciously, "but I hear shocking things about young Townsend. He was ejected from Oxford and has spent much of the time since in *France*."

Mrs. Brotherton clutched her lace fichu. "Among those savages who murdered their king?"

"I believe he returned to England before that," John admitted with some reluctance. "But his behavior and that of his friends has been the talk of London. And he collects pictures."

"What's wrong with that?" Eleanor asked. "Gentlemen of the highest rank are cognoscenti of art."

"Portraits of one's ancestors are all very well," John said, only a hint of discomfort on his bland features revealing that he had no idea what she was talking about. "But word at the

Corn Exchange this morning is that his taste runs to indecent subjects. I will say no more in front of ladies." That was so like John, to hint at interesting news and then refuse to repeat it. "His guardian is with him, a Mr. Max Quinton. Said to be a very sound man who has kept the estate in excellent condition."

Against her better judgment, Eleanor wanted to hear more.

"I don't know any Quintons." Elizabeth knew the peerage by heart and dismissed anyone who wasn't in it with a sniff." If young Townsend calls, I shall not receive him. He sounds like a poor influence for Caroline."

John frowned. "I don't think we can refuse the acquaintance altogether. He will be our neighbor. I shall call at Longford Hall and determine whether he is fit to be introduced to my mother. And sister."

Mrs. Brotherton's cold, handsome features creased into a rare smile. "Dearest John. What would I do without you?"

John returned from Longford with the news that Robert Townsend's three fellow expellees from Oxford had joined him for his birthday celebrations, which were to include a grand ball. Although two of them were of negligible, even undesirable birth, the third was Viscount Kendal.

"The Earl of Windermere's heir." Trust Cousin Elizabeth to know. "Quite an eligible *parti*. Caroline may put up her hair and attend the assembly. As long as she gives me no reason to change my mind."

"Will you stay for the ball, Eleanor?" Caro begged. "It won't be fun with just Mama as my chaperone."

Eleanor looked up the date. Three more weeks of possible encounters with Max Quinton. Her instinct was to make an excuse and leave immediately. But she had little confidence in Caro's ability to maintain good behavior without help. She stiffened her spine. If she let Max Quinton drive her away again, she admitted he still had the power to affect her. She had every confidence in her ability to meet him again with polite mutual indifference. To do otherwise would be irrational.

"I had intended to leave that week, but my father won't miss me if I remain in Somerset an extra day or two."

Max had come to the guardianship late. In exchange for a fee, he'd overseen the estate for several years on behalf of the previous incumbent, a distant cousin. Upon the latter's death he'd been appointed guardian for the last two years of Robert's minority. Since the boy, having been ejected from Oxford, was in Europe doing a truncated Grand Tour, his skills in loco parentis hadn't been much required or tested.

Now he found himself surrounded by youth, undisciplined boys whose Parisian junkets had ended when the French political situation slid into chaos. Despite their Latin tags, French phrases, and worldly knowledge of culture and politics, the boys still made Max think of a quartet of colts: handsome and bumptious. Colts with access to the dangerous toys of strong drink, cards, and dice.

Like most young animals, they needed fresh air and exercise, and this, in the declining days of his influence, Max was determined Robert and his friends would have. Not incidentally, calls around the neighborhood would bring Max into company with Eleanor Hardwick.

Finally, after five years, he'd met her again and no, it had not gone well. He'd made no headway at all in explaining what had happened, let alone excusing it. The trouble was, his actions were inexcusable. When Sir George had maliciously offered a pony to any officer who'd seduce his prissy cousin-in-law into a kiss, Max had been indifferent, his mild disgust drowned by Lord Egremont's claret. When the gathered competitors had raised the stakes and each contributed his own twenty-five guineas to the pot, he'd been somewhat interested. At that time sports had been of overwhelming interest and women little. Marriage had been something he saw in an indeterminate future. His time was consumed by responsibilities: arranging the future of his younger brothers and sisters; turning his late father's small estate into a flourishing enterprise.

But one look at Eleanor Hardwick and he was in. He'd wanted to kiss her more than he'd wanted to win the Petworth Stakes and that was saying a lot. Just as importantly, he *didn't* want any of the other men to win. That should have tipped him off to his feelings. The surge of annoyance that possessed him when he contemplated any of the officers managing so much as a peck on her cheek should have alerted him that his bachelor days were numbered. But he was a man's man and knew nothing of finer feelings. It took the best part of a week before he realized he'd found the lady of his dreams and marriage became his highest priority.

But when she'd discovered the wager, it was all over. In one interview and half a dozen letters he'd tried to explain that his intentions had changed. A fruitless endeavor. She wouldn't even hear him out. When she pushed him into the river he'd thought he was finally over her, that the image haunting him for so long had been dispelled by cold water and frigid scorn. It took only dry clothing to shake his certainty.

Meanwhile, he had three weeks left as guardian to Robert Townsend, three short weeks to drum some sense into the boy's clever but senseless head. He summoned him to the estate office to discuss some issues with the tenantry that had arisen since their arrival.

As usual when business was the subject, Robert looked bored. "Whatever you think is best, Max. You know better than I."

"I do know better, but that's because I've been running the estate. After your birthday the decisions will be yours. You have a competent steward, but there's no substitute for the knowledge and attention of the owner."

Robert sighed and pretended to listen, but clearly his mind was elsewhere. After half an hour, he stood up. "I can't leave the fellows alone any longer," he said. "What kind of a host would I be? They're waiting for me to make up a table of whist."

"Low stakes, I trust." Max knew he should hold his tongue. The more he harangued Robert about his gaming losses, the more stubborn the latter became.

"Don't be a bore, Max. Damian's the only one of us with any money anyway. At least until I escape your pinchpenny ways. Marcus has been studying the odds. Hoyle on piquet, of course, but he's also made his own calculations, especially for vingt-et-un and hazard. We're all going to make a fortune."

Robert wasn't a bad boy, but his upbringing under his previous guardian had blended neglect and indulgence. Since his expulsion from Oxford he'd run in a wild set. Max cast about for a distraction. "We'll have to find better ways to entertain your friends than dice and cards. A pity the stables are so poor here, but we should call on some neighbors."

"Country society! Men with red faces who talk about horses, and their devilishly plain daughters. None of them ever reads a book or travels farther than Bath."

"You didn't find Miss Brotherton plain," Max said, rather desperately.

Robert's face brightened. "She's a beauty. But she's a lady, Max. The kind of girl one has to wed, if you get my meaning."

"Indeed, Robert. You can't, er, dally with Miss Brotherton, and I don't suppose you're looking to marry at your age." He had an inspiration. "But a flirtation with a pretty girl of gentle birth can be a very pleasant experience and a way to idle away the time you must spend in the country."

He brushed aside a twinge of compunction. Caro Brotherton had a brother and a mother to watch over her, not to mention her very own dragon, Miss Eleanor Hardwick. Trying to get by the guards would give Robert something to do other than gaming. And Max was happy to help, by distracting the dragon.

Calling the next day on Caro's friend, the novel-reading Lucy Markham, Eleanor and Caro found Lucy, the younger Markham children, and their governess in the garden, entertaining Robert Townsend and his three friends. Since Caro naturally wished to remain in such enthralling company, Eleanor went into the house alone to call on Mrs. Markham. The Markhams were friendly souls, fond of visiting and being visited. The morning room was populated by several ladies and, looking quite at home and the center of attention, Max Quinton.

After the expected flurry of greetings among the ladies, her hostess presented Mr. Quinton to Eleanor.

"Miss Hardwick and I are old friends," he said, unabashed by the cold look she shot at him.

All the ladies looked interested, the younger and unmarried ones faintly annoyed.

"We've met."

"Once we knew each other quite well."

She was infuriated to feel her cheeks grow hot. His sly look told her that by "once" he meant on one particular occasion. The dastard.

"I am happy to meet you on dry land," he continued. "Pray join me on this sofa. I shall feel much safer if you are seated."

Miss Markham looked baffled. "Whatever can you mean, Mr. Quinton?"

"Last time I met Miss Hardwick I suffered an unfortunate accident."

"And the time before, I did," Eleanor snapped under her breath. She turned her attention firmly to her hostess. "How are you, ma'am? Over the sniffles, I trust. Summer colds can be difficult to shake."

"Quite recovered, dear Miss Hardwick. Thank you for asking. Pray come and sit beside me and Mrs. Walpole and tell me how Mrs. Brotherton does. Will you take tea?"

Her hostess's intervention was on her eldest daughter's behalf. Miss Markham appeared highly interested in Mr. Quinton, and her cousin, Miss Ansty, was her rival for his attentions. Sitting between the two young ladies, Max seemed to be enjoying himself hugely. Luckily they had watchful parents to stop them falling for the seductive blandishments that she knew only too well he'd possessed. Still possessed. She despised herself for still finding him appealing.

He was a man comfortable in his own skin. A countryman through and through, he would never be mistaken for a man of fashion. His broadcloth coat in pine green and buff buckskin breeches were plain and only discreetly hinted at his powerful figure. As Eleanor had reason to know, the hints did not deceive. He responded to the sallies of his youthful admirers with sense laced with humor that would charm the birds out of the trees, or a lady out of her virtue.

Mrs. Markham's chatter about the ailments, major and minor, real and imaginary, of their neighbors taxed Eleanor's intellect so little she found herself sneaking blink-length glances in his direction far too often. Eventually her luck ran out and he caught her looking. For an endless moment his blue gaze held hers with the illusion of warmth and longing. For illusion it was. Max's affection had never been anything else.

She turned her neck sharply. Mrs. Markham had said something that required a reply. "How very disagreeable, ma'am."

Unfortunately she'd lost the thread of the conversation and failed to notice that the subject had changed from weaknesses of the body to those of the heart.

"Oh no! A most happy occasion. Her mother informs me it is a love match."

"A love match!" Mrs. Walpole, the parson's wife, entered the lists with gusto. "They always lead to trouble."

"Surely not," said Mrs. Markham. "I would desire them above all for my girls."

"Love is all very well, but may not last. A woman is well advised to look for a gentleman who is able to keep her and her children in a suitable state. And a man needs a wife of sense who can forward his endeavors." Mrs. Walpole, Eleanor remembered, was the daughter of a bishop and fully intended that her husband should attain an equal status. Or higher. She suspected that a diocese was too small a pond for the lady. She desired a *see*. "You seem a young woman of sense, Miss Hardwick. What is your opinion?"

"I believe all our actions should be governed by rationality," Eleanor said.

Mrs. Markham shook her head. "Naturally I don't advocate a rash or unequal match, but marriage without mutual esteem . . ."

"Mutual esteem is one thing but love is dangerous." The parson's wife delivered her opinion in a stentorian manner that would not have disgraced her husband's pulpit. Her raised voice—and the magic word love—attracted the attention of the younger ladies and their quarry. "What say you, Mr. Quinton? Pray give us the gentleman's perspective. Do you not agree with Miss Hardwick that matrimony is best entered rationally?"

He sent Eleanor a quizzical look, before answering the other lady. "I cannot be held to be an expert on the topic, ma'am."

"Would you not wish a wife to assist you in your ambitions?"

"I'm not sure what you have in mind. I am a horse breeder and I cannot see how a wife would help me find a Derby winner, unless she was an expert on horseflesh and an authority on the bloodlines of the great stallions."

"I am ever so fond of horses," Miss Markham interjected. Eleanor doubted the girl, who had a nervous disposition, had ever mounted anything more spirited than a fat pony.

"Pish," Mrs. Walpole said. "That's not what I mean. I'm sure Mr. Quinton knows his own business and needs no interference from a wife. I would never think of telling Mr. Walpole what to think about the Scriptures or how to write his sermon. But a wise wife can help a gentleman cultivate the favor of those with influence."

Misses Ansty and Markham tried to look wise and capable of cultivating influence.

"You make an excellent point," he said. "Five years ago in Sussex, I had the good fortune to meet the Earl of Egremont, whose Assassin won the Derby in '82. Exactly at the same time and place I met Miss Hardwick."

Four pairs of female eyes turned with fascination or resentment in Eleanor's direction. "A mere coincidence, I assure you," she said, infuriated by the heat in her cheeks. "I had nothing to do with Mr. Quinton's meeting Lord Egremont."

"I didn't mean that you did," he said with spurious innocence. What *did* he mean, then?

Mrs. Walpole charged back into the fray. "It's high time a man like you was wed."

"I agree." The four pairs of eyes swiveled back to him and

grew round. Eleanor forced her hands to rest still in her lap and her face to remain bland. "I would like to be wed," he continued, "but I haven't yet found a lady who both shares my sentiments about marriage and returns them."

Miss Markham sighed. Miss Ansty, daringly, placed a hand on his arm. "Oh, Mr. Quinton!" she said in an unnaturally husky voice. "Please explain yourself."

Max, looking odiously smug, visibly relaxed between his two faithful handmaidens. "I wouldn't look for a lady to know more about horses than I do . . ."

"How could she?" Miss Ansty said with a triumphant look at her cousin.

" . . . But I would want her to be interested in the subject, better still share my feelings and opinions."

Eleanor thought of her father and his obsession with tracing the antediluvian flora of the ancient world. She wasn't sure the tedium of the subject hadn't hastened her mother to the grave. It certainly drove her, Eleanor, out of the house.

"How charming for her, Mr. Quinton," she said sweetly. And refused to remember that she'd enjoyed hearing him talk about his work, displaying intelligence and knowledge without long-winded self-satisfaction.

His eyes twinkled. "I hope so."

"A lady likes to be listened to, also," said Mrs. Walpole.

"And I would wish to wed a lady who was able to converse on her own business with sense and intelligence."

"Your condescension overwhelms me," Eleanor said.

"No need for that, Miss Hardwick. I have the highest respect for the fair sex."

Eleanor's jaw clenched. Smiles and soft sighs told her that Max held the other ladies in the palm of his hand.

"For truly," he concluded, "what I seek is the marriage of true minds. I will settle for nothing less." His gaze passed around the company, settling only briefly on her, not long enough to draw attention. His expression held such sincerity that she didn't know what to think. A craven desire to believe him fought the reason that told her he was applying his cynical powers of persuasion on her, and every other woman present.

"What of fortune, sir?" asked the practical parson's wife.

"Since my own wealth is modest, it would ill become me to demand more from my wife."

"And beauty?" asked Miss Ansty, the prettier of the two cousins. "Do you seek beauty in a wife?"

Max pretended to give the matter grave thought, "pretend" being the correct word. Eleanor realized she knew him well enough to detect the approach of an outrageous statement. "It is of the utmost importance," he said, "that I find a lady beautiful. She may not be handsome to every eye, but to me she must be lovely, or how could I live with her in the mutual joy that is the essence of marriage?"

Mrs. Markham looked slightly shocked. The girls looked confused.

"Mr. Quinton," said the vicar's wife, "despite the good sense you display, I should remind you that there are unmarried ladies present." But she was smiling and Eleanor found herself wishing the lady well in her ambition to be Mrs. Bishop Walpole. Despite her wonderfully sensible views on love, she guessed that the Walpoles were a contented couple.

One of the few. Eleanor, being a reasonable woman, would never deny that *some* marriages were happy. Merely that the odds were unfavorable.

"I apologize, ma'am," Max replied. "But I'd like to say that Mr. Walpole is a very fortunate man."

The stalwart vicar's wife almost simpered. Max Quinton had made another conquest, despite a reference to the marriage bed such as Eleanor had never heard in mixed company. Unwillingly she was a little thrilled that the object of this slightly indecent remark was herself. For now his eyes settled on her. He was sending the message that he still found her desirable, despite her unpretty thirty year-old face. She reached for her teacup, stirring in more sugar than she usually liked.

No, she wasn't shocked, but she did blush. She blushed for the memories that gripped her of the gardens at Petworth Park, when she and Max had walked down to the lake during the ball that marked the conclusion of a week of horseracing. The details of that hour were a blur; all she remembered were her own feelings. For once, recollection of delight overcame the bitterness of the aftermath. The intensity in his unwavering gaze evoked the ecstasy of that summer night. She wanted to close her eyes and absorb the scent of roses, the ripples of water in the moonlight, the song of the nightingale. She wished she was alone so she could revel in the heat that set flesh and skin glowing and swirled to a delicious ache in her secret core. She yearned to be touched and filled and, not for the first time, inwardly railed against the injustice that forbade satisfaction unless it came with the bondage of matrimony.

What would these innocent girls and proper ladies think

if they knew that one of their number, Mrs. Brotherton's upright spinster cousin, had once, in a moment of madness, participated in the "mutual joy" Mr. Quinton referred to? *With* Mr. Quinton.

To her disgust, she sat on the sofa in Mrs. Markham's drawing room and wanted him still. Had she no pride? Remember what happened afterward, she told herself sternly. Remember the next morning's humiliation.

Five years earlier, Max had wanted her far more than he wanted the two hundred guineas in Sir George Ashdown's betting pool for kissing his wife's prissy, irritating spinster cousin. As he quickly learned, Eleanor was a thorough delight. Not at all irritating, far from prissy, and he couldn't imagine why she had remained a spinster.

Well, she wouldn't remain one for long. Max wasn't a rich man; the estate he'd inherited from his father was small. But its location near Newmarket was an advantage for a horse breeder. He'd made several sales during the week at Petworth, including one to Lord Egremont himself. With the promise of future patronage, he was in a position to take a wife. And while he wasn't altogether happy about its source, the two hundred would be helpful for a man starting a family.

An ill-fated decision. As he learned later, ladies did not appreciate being the subjects of wagers. Those gathered in Mrs. Markham's drawing room today would certainly disapprove. What a fool he'd been. He should at least have told Eleanor about the bet.

His sin of omission was only the first mistake he made the

night of the Petworth ball. He had tossed back another glass of wine before inviting Miss Hardwick to sit out their next dance and walk in the gardens instead. He wasn't drunk, but any man needed a little Dutch courage to propose marriage.

There could be few places on earth more beautiful than Petworth Park by moonlight. No expense of money or skill had been spared in making it an earthly paradise. Benches in plenty were provided for the weary visitor to rest while he admired the vistas. Had Max and Eleanor been sitting on cold stone or hard wooden boards, decorum might have been maintained. But his genius discovered a grass bank surrounded by shrubbery, including a tall scrambling rose bush possessing profuse white blooms of peculiar sweetness.

A proposal and a kiss, most likely in that order. That was his plan.

The scent of roses and the more intoxicating perfume of a warm woman. Dry grass beneath him, scythed to the texture of moss, competing with the peachy smoothness of her cheeks. The taste of her lips sending his head spinning. And the headier discovery that his hunger was reciprocated. Speech withered, desire dominated action.

A moment's silence in the room heightened the sound of Eleanor's skirts shifting as she reached for her teacup, drawing him deeper into the memory of that night.

The rustle of silken gown and fine linen pushed aside were lost in the sweeter sound of Eleanor's breathy sighs. Soft cries cheered his quest for the tenderest skin that marked the approach to heaven, her warm, wet welcoming center. Her fiery, innocent responses sent him soaring and ruined him for other women. He'd never once intended to seduce her, until the enchantment of the evening pulverized the scruples of a gentleman. Later he assuaged his guilt with the certainty that she had been as eager, as overcome with desire as he.

Now he sat in Mrs. Markham's drawing room sending Eleanor Hardwick improper messages. Each time she blushed and avoided his eye fueled his courage and a new determination. Winning her back was more important than any race he'd ever run.

CHAPTER THREE

"**M**iss Hardwick, Miss Brotherton! What a delightful surprise."

Max vaulted over the stile into the field, Robert Townsend at his heels.

"I shouldn't be astonished, but I confess I am," Eleanor said. "How did you find us in this obscure field?"

"We saw your hats floating above the hedge and came to offer you company."

Her hand went to the brim of the huge straw confection, impractical for such an expedition, but she did love it. She was glad she'd worn it today. Caro, who had teased her about it, exchanged grins with Robert.

"Today we are in search of early blackberries, not company," she said.

"How extraordinary! Robert and I are on the same errand."

"To make a tart for your supper, no doubt."

"Just so, though I believe the cook will do the making."

"You won't gather many without a basket."

Max looked around him. "I knew I'd forgotten something. Robert! Did you remember your basket?"

"Not I," replied his ward, who was freeing Caro's skirts from a bramble. Eleanor sighed, fearing the little minx had got herself caught on purpose, and made sure it involved the revelation of her ankles and a good measure of calf.

"Robert may share mine," Caro said.

"And in exchange," Robert replied, "I shall show you the place for the best berries."

"And how would you know?" Eleanor asked, assuming her disapproving chaperone face. "A childhood memory, perhaps?"

"That, and an unerring eye for beauty." The boy stared at Caro's ankle for several seconds before dropping the petticoat he'd unhooked from the last thorn.

"May I go with Mr. Townsend, please Eleanor?"

"Don't go too far, and stay in sight," Eleanor said.

The youngsters moved off in search of the riper fruit, always a few bushes away, leaving Eleanor with Max. Although she was now accustomed to his presence, she'd always seen him in a group, never alone.

"We seem to be meeting everywhere these days," Eleanor said.

"Inevitable when visiting a country neighborhood."

"You and your party attended both morning service and evensong on Sunday. Impressive piety in a group of young men."

"Mr. Walpole is a fine preacher, don't you agree?"

"I do. Yet I had the impression their full attention was not on the sermon." She strongly suspected the high-walled

Townsend pew had sheltered some surreptitious dicing. "I was even more surprised," she continued, "to meet you all when we called on Mrs. Coyle. A parson's elderly widow and her spinster daughter are not generally the preferred company of handsome young men." Miss Coyle was notorious for her good natured but inane chatter. She and Max had exchanged secret smiles during one of the lady's particularly impressive flights of nonsense.

He grinned shamelessly. "Just doing our neighborly duty."

"Very praiseworthy I am sure. And it was by chance that our visits coincided?"

"Pure coincidence. And a most happy one."

She knew it was not a coincidence and couldn't help but be pleased. The past two weeks had recalled race week at Petworth, the happy part, not the painful end. Those had been exhilarating days, a whirl of picnics and dances, all of them spent in a state of heightened awareness. She'd acquired eyes in the back of her head. Max had only to enter a room for her to know it. His proximity, at the distance of a dozen feet or two, drove the blood coursing through her veins and all rational thought out of her head. It was often two feet, for the moment he noticed her he'd make for her side, ignoring other guests to the point of discourtesy, his lazy smile only for her. She'd lived in a cloud of sensation, an ocean of feelings. Abandonment of reason had cost her dearly.

Yet it wasn't the same. He still approached her at every opportunity. Their discourse was pleasant and impersonal, such as anyone might overhear without raising an eyebrow. Age must have lent her greater wisdom. Because they had no shared future, she could forget Max's faults and enjoy his company—always good company—without danger to her peace of mind. Why he made a point of seeking her out scarcely mattered. She'd give him no encouragement so he couldn't be misled.

"What are you really doing here today?" she asked, with a mock frown. "Inspecting the fences or some such fascinating thing, I suppose. Tell me the truth."

Max was making progress. He'd swear she'd greeted his arrival with pleasure and she may have blushed beneath the ridiculous hat, adorned with a bewildering display of ribbons and whatnot that no normal man could possibly be expected to sort out. But it mattered not. Eleanor had the presence to carry off any fashion excess and still look infinitely desirable. The hat could be removed. As could the cream-colored shawl and the crisp bright gown—green today—that set off her shining dark hair.

"Actually you're not far wrong. Robert has been enduring a lecture on drainage."

The creases in her forehead dissolved and the fine gray eyes grew warm with amusement. Around him the sounds of birdsong and insects faded away on the breeze. Her lips parted and he bent his head as though to inhale her moist, sweet breath. He was enthralled, ensorcelled, his mind empty of all but one thought, to kiss Eleanor Hardwick again.

She turned her head aside and stepped away, uttering an unladylike oath when a bramble pulled at her skirt. Unlike Caro, she freed herself without fuss and started picking fruit.

"You never told me you had a ward," she said.

"A recent acquisition. My guardianship is mostly a matter of form. I attend to his estate." Finally he had Eleanor to himself, without the neighborhood busybodies listening to every word. He didn't want to waste it speaking of Robert.

"I'm told you are good at it."

"Just doing my duty, and at some profit to myself. I am paid for my trouble."

"I'm glad to hear it."

"I've never pretended to be a wealthy man."

"I know a good many gentlemen of different degrees of fortune and it has always appeared to me that the happiest are those who are busiest. Being born to a healthy independence can be a disadvantage if it leads to idleness."

He watched her toss fruit into her basket with easy competence. "You like to be busy yourself, I think."

"I am a practical woman. Some would say I have a managing disposition, and they don't mean it as a compliment."

Max recalled Sir George Ashdown's sneers, definitely not a topic he wished to raise. "They are wrong. No one who wears a contrivance like that on her head can be entirely practical."

She peeped at him from beneath the exaggerated brim. "Hats are my greatest weakness."

"Your only weakness?" He waited for her answer through a long spool of silence, broken by a shriek.

Robert was running across the field being bombarded with blackberries by the hotly pursuing Caro. So much for not being interrupted.

"What an unruly pair of children they are," he said. "Your little cousin's gown will be stained."

Eleanor groaned. "I had to smuggle her into the house after she fell in the river to protect her from her mother's wrath." She stopped her fruit picking and looked at him, scrunching up her nose. His heart lurched. He'd forgotten that look of amused puzzlement. "Elizabeth Brotherton seems to think children should be born with tastes and habits like great-grandmothers of more than usual propriety. She should never have been a mother."

"You're fond of the girl, aren't you?"

"There's such sweetness and fun in her. How she manages to remain so delightful when she's been at odds with her parent most of her life, I don't know. If she can get through the wild age, she will grow up to be a remarkable woman. Don't tell the others, but Caro is perhaps my favorite of all my young cousins."

"And how many do you have?"

"Dozens and dozens. I may have been an only child, but both my parents came from families of excessive fruitfulness." She spoke with droll exaggeration but he caught an off-key note.

"Did you miss having brothers and sisters? I have two of each and there were times when our house seemed overly full, even without the constant comings and goings of visitors. I can't imagine a quiet house."

"My father's house is isolated."

The simple words spoke volumes. Eleanor was a warm and gregarious creature. No wonder she spent her time visiting, lavishing her affection on her young relations. He realized this was one of the most personal conversations he'd ever had with her. Their previous meetings had taken place in the hectic atmosphere of race week. They'd laughed and flirted and shared the superficial information of new acquaintants. Everything about her had enchanted him, but physical desire had been uppermost in his mind. In the end, his lack of control over his own urges had ruined things. He should have wooed her properly, as a lady, discovered more about her own feelings and concerns.

"Your father is a clergyman. They don't usually lead quiet lives."

"It's a small parish."

"I've never visited Lancashire. What are the people like there?"

"Much like people everywhere, I imagine."

"Did your mother die long ago?"

"Yes."

The shorter her answers to his probing, the more convinced he became that she was hiding something. He didn't know what, but there had to be a reason why an intelligent and handsome woman had remained unwed, despite being ideally suited to family life. He stepped back, physically and mentally. He mustn't rush his fences this time.

"I owe you an apology," he said.

"Why? I mean, yes. But it's all past now and not worth talking about."

"I think it is, but not now. Instead I'm going to extend my deepest thanks to all the men in England for being blind idiots."

"How so?" she asked warily.

"Because they have allowed you to remain unwed."

"At my own wish, not theirs." She seemed annoyed at the suggestion she'd never had an offer.

"It makes me feel better now I realize that I was just one of a legion you rejected."

"Not so many, but one or two. And you were the only one who ever tested my resolve." His breath caught. Such an admission was surely significant. "Anyway," she continued briskly, as though she hadn't just sent his heart tumbling. "Are you going to help me pick blackberries? I don't count on Caro coming home with enough to fill a single tartlet."

He reached over her shoulder to retrieve a particularly large specimen from a far branch. "I prefer to eat as I pick, especially when I find a beauty. Delicious."

"Unfair! The biggest and ripest are always the farthest away."

"That is why you should never go blackberry picking without a gentleman in attendance. How lucky for you that we happened along."

They worked for a while, speaking idly and only of the task at hand, until the basket was full. Eleanor proved an indefatigable forager.

"Is that enough? May we rest from our labors? I see a shady spot under that oak where we can sit and talk of graves and worms and epitaphs."

She caught his Shakespearean allusion and laughed. "What a charming invitation! Let me just pick that last bunch. I swear they are the best ones I've seen."

"That's the sixth time you've said that. I'll get them. It's too far for you to reach." He spoke too late. She stretched across the breadth of the bramble patch and gave a little cry.

"You've hurt yourself!" He pushed back the ruffle that fell from the elbow-length sleeve. Tiny spots of bloods punctuated the white skin of her inner arm. With infinite care he dabbed up the blood with his handkerchief. "Are you in pain?"

"It's nothing."

"Here," he said softly. "I'll kiss it better."

She tried to pull away but he wouldn't let her, retaining a gentle but undeniable hold on her elbow and wrist. His lips traced the angry red line of the scratch. He took his time about it, relishing the soft skin impregnated with a subtle floral fragrance. All too soon he reached her wrist, but he had no intention of stopping. He prolonged his pleasure, lingering at the tender joint. She gasped when he let his tongue emerge to enjoy the taste of salt and blackberry, but she didn't struggle. So he held the hand, liberally stained with purple juice, in both of his, nuzzled the palm and took the tips of her strong slender fingers, one by one, into his mouth.

"Max," she murmured. Finally she'd used his Christian name. "My hand is dirty."

"It tastes sweet," he said, replacing the forefinger with the middle one.

"Here," she said, sounding a little desperate. With her free hand she grabbed a berry from the basket. "If you must eat."

He raised his head from her hand but otherwise made no other movement except to part his lips. He held his breath, his heart hammering wildly. The fruit glistened in the sunlight before she inserted it into his waiting mouth. Sweet and tart, just like her. Even more than the fruit he relished the avid look on her face as she watched him swallow.

"Thank you," he said softly. "Now let me find one of the biggest and ripest for you."

He'd already spotted his quarry on the bush, out of the corner of his eye. He plucked it carefully and pressed it into her slightly open mouth. She chewed convulsively and a tiny driblet of purple seeped out. Quick as a wink he took the lush lower lip between both of his and sucked off the juice. And before he knew it, he was kissing Eleanor again and she was kissing him back.

Standing a foot or so apart, only their lips touched, and their hands. He'd never released the one he'd so thoroughly kissed. One corner of his brain was urging him to seize her, embrace her, press her against the growing evidence of his desire, throw her to the ground and possess her. Only knowing that haste had once led him to lose her stayed his passion. Stayed, not dispelled.

He wanted her body, heart, and soul, forever. Her body he'd won before and he sensed from her response that he could do so again. But her heart was hidden behind defenses he'd never suspected existed, because he'd never taken the trouble to find out. As for her soul, he'd bruised it badly when he'd betrayed her trust with that foolish bet. He still had work to do.

He kissed her gently, their lips moving together soft and sweet. It wasn't a deep kiss but a slow investigation of taste and texture, a scouting trip with the promise of a full exploration. Max let lust fall away as he devoted his mind to the joy of a simple kiss with the woman he loved.

Still, she was the first to break contact, not him. He wasn't that saintly. "Caro," she said in strangled voice, blinking foolishly. Since her back was to the open field, Max had an excellent view over her shoulder of Caro and Robert, hands clasped and about to kiss.

"Robert!" he shouted. His first thought was that Eleanor should not know. If she did, she'd keep Caro away from Robert and their frequent meetings would stop. He needed time, much more time, to win her over.

Chapter Four

It was a long time since Eleanor had dressed for a ball with such anticipation. Five years to be precise. By chance Robert Townsend's twenty-first birthday fell on the anniversary of the Petworth militia ball. She was somewhat disgusted with herself that the cause of her excitement was the same in both cases, the pleasure of dancing with the same man.

However hard she tried to think like a sensible woman of thirty years, she couldn't stop feeling like a girl as young and foolish as Caro. Her body swayed in time with imagined music, drawing a remonstrance from the maid who was lacing up her stays. She twirled in front of the mirror, admiring the swish and rustle of her favorite blue silk gown, then picked out the steps of a lively gavotte, just to relax her feet into the matching dancing slippers embroidered with seed pearls.

Her heart felt light. She hadn't thought it possible, yet at this moment she felt no anger toward Max. He'd made a mistake. Everyone made them, especially gentlemen. Normally tolerant of human foibles, she'd believed him unpardonable. Perhaps there was a lesson here, that anyone deserved forgiveness—once.

"You look beautiful, Eleanor." Caro gave her a hug that took Eleanor's breath away when she joined the family downstairs.

"Caroline! You'll crush your dress." Elizabeth Brotherton was ever ready to spoil a moment of enjoyment.

In a way she was right. Caro's gown of fine white gauze would crush easily. She was so excited that her vibrant red curls already threatened to come loose from their pretty arrangement of satin ribbon and pearls. Eleanor was quite certain the girl would return from her first ball with her pristine kid slippers and gloves soiled and worn. But who could object? Caro's youthful glee was infectious and certain to charm the stuffiest of sticklers.

Except her own mother. Mrs. Brotherton was dressed with impeccable taste in her favorite lavender. Eleanor would bet her entire fortune on the certainty that Elizabeth would come home in as perfect a state as she'd left in, flawlessly pressed, coiffed, and scented by the sweet lavender powder she favored.

Eleanor herself strove for no such undisturbed state. No normal woman could survive an evening's dancing entirely unruffled. Her stomach fluttered dangerously at the anticipation of another cause of ruffling. Since the blackberry expedition she had spent far too much time dwelling on that kiss, and she was fairly sure—almost sure—that she would let it be repeated tonight. What else that meant for her future she wasn't certain.

"What a splendid ball," Eleanor said when Max claimed

her for the first set. "I am impressed that a mere man could arrange things so well."

"Thank you. I've never acted as host on such an occasion. And I will not do so again. Not at Longford, at least. As of this morning I relinquish all control over Robert and the Townsend estate."

"How long will you stay?" she asked, as they moved through the dance.

"That depends."

"On what?"

"On whether Robert allows me to remain his guest." His lazy smile sent a different message.

"Ah, you fear summary ejection. Have you been such a cruel, strict guardian then?"

Max turned to the lady on his other side. Eleanor felt her toes curl and a foolish grin stretch her lips. In evening clothes of gray and deep red he looked far handsomer than any gentleman in the room. "He and the boys intend to leave here in a day or two," he said, once the dance brought him back to her side. "He's not cut out for country life and chafes for London."

Eleanor looked at Caro, who was gazing at Robert as they danced. "It's probably just as well," she said. "Caro will be sad, but they are both too young to marry."

"Worrying about your charge?"

"She's not mine tonight. Her mother is present."

"All the more attention for others, then," he whispered, as the movement of the dance drew them apart again.

"I'll never be host at Longford again," Max said a minute later. "But I have my own house, near Newmarket. It's not as large as this one but I hope you would like it."

"That's one part of England I've never visited," she said, trying to sound indifferent. "For some reason I have no relations there. I would like to visit Cambridge. The colleges are said to be very fine." Once again the movements of the dance separated them.

"Eleanor," he said softly, when they came back together. "Are we going to spend this evening discussing the beauties and antiquities of England?"

"I generally find travel to be a fine topic when one is traveling through a country dance."

"In that case," he said, "I hope you will reserve a later set for me and we can forget the dance and walk outside. The gardens are very lovely at this time of year."

Her heart hammered and her breath increased. A tingling of her lips anticipated that kiss she'd promised herself. Just a kiss. And she wouldn't go far from the house. This time she was not going to lose control of herself.

"There's nothing like an evening walk," she said. "Meanwhile you may tell me about the fen country. What is it like?"

"Very flat." His smile made her wish the promised *later set* was now. She felt herself drowning in a heated gaze that seemed incongruous in such limpid blue eyes.

The ball was endless. Max fretted through half a dozen sets and the tedium of supper. In a house filled with the cream of Somerset gentry, there was only one person whose company he desired. Finally it came time for his promised dance with Eleanor. She, ravishing in blue, stood with her cousin, the impossibly unpleasant Mrs. Brotherton.

"Will you do me the honor, Miss Hardwick?"

"I would be pleased." Her demure answer was belied by the smoke in her gray eyes. "But I find the room a trifle overwarm."

"In that case, may I suggest a stroll under the stars?"

"This has been the longest evening of my life," he said once he had her on his arm. "My job as Robert's guardian is supposed to be over today, but the wretched boy keeps disappearing, leaving me as sole host. I'm afraid he's dicing in the stables with the other youngsters. The three of them are probably fleecing the rustics, as Lithgow so charmingly puts it."

"As long as no one's fleecing Caro of her virtue, I don't care."

"Good God! I hope not. Why would you think such a thing?" Surely Robert wouldn't? Max beat aside his uneasiness at the suggestion.

"Just a joke, a poor one. My duty is to prevent Caro and her mother from being at odds. She's dancing with Lord Kendal now, which will please Cousin Elizabeth. I don't really believe Mr. Townsend would seduce her."

The light remark fell into a pool of silence, pregnant with meaning and memories. "Do you know what day this is?" he asked.

"Of course I do, but I didn't expect you would."

A number of guests had come out to seek the cool of the night, but Eleanor and Max were far enough from the house to be out of the earshot of others. Max halted and gazed down at her face, pale and lovely against the dark halo of her hair. He itched to frame the soft cheeks in his palms, delineate the high cheekbones with his thumbs, kiss the elegant nose whose slight prominence gave her face such character. He contented himself with taking her hand. She did not pull away.

"Not a day goes by when I do not remember that night." A wisp of a breath was her only response. Max chose to find hope in her silence. "When you returned my letters I despaired, but I never wholly gave up. I always hoped we would meet again."

As he spoke he saw pain in her eyes that squeezed at his heart. "Why?" she asked. He bent to hear the repeated word. "Why?" For his forthright Eleanor to speak so softly was another testament to how badly he'd hurt her. "It's not so much the original contest. I know men can be foolish, especially when they drink too much. But why did you boast about it to Sir George Ashdown?"

"Boast? To an oaf like Ashdown? I did nothing of the kind."

"He told me you had. In the carriage on the way home from Petworth. He said the officers of the regiment had a contest to see who could win a kiss from me. When you claimed the prize, you implied that you'd won far more. I've never been so humiliated in my life."

"Ashdown lied."

"But you did win two hundred pounds."

"When we returned from the lake that night, Ashdown asked me if I'd fulfilled the terms of the contest—to kiss you, nothing more—and I told him I had. To my shame, I took the money. I'm not a rich man and I was intending to be wed. To you. But I promise you Eleanor, I swear on every scrap of honor I ever possessed, that nothing I said to Ashdown can have given him the idea that we did anything more that night than exchange a kiss. I told him I would call the next morning to offer for your hand because I was in love with you."

"You said that?"

"My dearest Eleanor. I fell in love with you that week and that night I thought you felt the same." Joy seized his heart. Eleanor and he had been victims of a misunderstanding. Now they could be happy.

She hadn't quite reached the same state of bliss. She was looking for answers. "Ashdown said he forced you to propose to me. That you were reluctant, but after much persuasion you agreed that you owed me marriage."

"Good God! No wonder you sent me away. Why would Ashdown play such a trick?"

"Because he is a horrible man and wanted to revenge himself on me. Poor Sylvia, his wife, has six children and still he would not leave her alone. I advised her to stand up to him, to refuse to let him into her bed for at least a few months. I knew he was angry with me for helping my cousin find a backbone, but I had no notion he could be so vicious. Where are we going?"

The last question was a response to Max's dragging her by the hand toward the shelter of a convenient shrubbery. "I'm not waiting another minute to kiss you."

She was not, thank heaven, reluctant. As soon as they were safely out of sight, she fell into his arms. They devoured each other with the same hunger they'd shared five years ago, almost to the hour. Yet it meant so much more this time, because he'd lost her and had found her again. The way her body strained into his was a gift that humbled him, the taste of her kiss a priceless treasure. Five years deprived of Eleanor made every fraction of a second in her presence infinitely precious.

His darling was a woman of powerful appetites beneath a serene exterior. There was nothing tentative or restrained about her embrace, not a trace of maidenly reluctance. She demanded, sucking his tongue into her mouth while emitting an animal purr from the depths of her throat. No puny ladylike creature she, with strong arms that snaked beneath his coats to caress his back, her fingers delicious fiery brands through the linen of his shirt. Why did women have to wear so many layers? his brain hazily wondered, as his own hands sought the ecstasy and comfort of skin and flesh and found only the sturdy cloth and bones of her stays. Finally, in desperation, he relinquished her mouth so that he could taste the long column of her neck, the expanse of chest, and the smooth firm breasts thrust upward for his delectation by the same corset that frustrated him elsewhere. Her head fell back to give him access and at the same time her hands grasped his satin-breeched buttocks and pulled his swelling cock against her center, grinding into him in time with her speeding breaths.

What a marriage they would have! What days and nights of delight!

He stopped trying to burrow beneath the lace edge of her gown to find her nipples. "Eleanor," he whispered. "Enough."

An incoherent moan of displeasure accompanied an attempt to find his lips again.

He put a few inches of air between them so his thoughts would no longer be scrambled by her touch. "Let us not repeat our mistakes. Before we go any further, let us set a wedding date."

She blinked in a flattering state of bedazzlement, shook her head a couple of times with resultant danger to the state of her coiffure, and then opened her mouth a couple of times as she formulated a speech that he hoped would run along the lines of *next week*.

"Are we betrothed?" she said.

He laughed. "I should know better than to take you for granted, my darling. Do you want me to propose on one knee?"

She waved aside the question, as though it was an irrelevance. "I'm not sure I wish to be married."

"What?" Max was outraged. "You just kissed me as no lady should kiss a man who is not her betrothed or, preferably, her husband."

"Don't be prissy, Max. We've done nothing that makes it essential we wed."

"I thought you'd forgiven me."

"I have."

"Five years ago, you were ready to marry me, until Ashdown interfered. Why not now?"

"Actually," she said, "I wasn't intending to wed you then, either."

"What?"

"Hush! Do you want to summon a crowd?"

With some difficulty, Max moderated his tone. "Do you mean to say you lay with me, you surrendered your virtue, with no intention of marrying me?"

"I'll admit I wasn't thinking very clearly that night. I was a little carried away. After it happened"—she smiled at the reminiscence in a way he could only characterize as lascivious—"I might have considered wedding you. Sir George Ashdown quickly squashed that idea."

Max felt the ground slipping out from under his feet. "Do you love me, Eleanor?" he asked, trying to bring the discussion back under control. "I loved you then and I love you now. You are the only woman I have ever loved, the only one I wish to marry and live with for the rest of my life." An astonishing and hurtful idea occurred to him. "Did you love me? Or was I merely a week's flirtation to be used and set aside?"

She took his hands in each of hers and looked up at him, her head tilted to one side. "I think I did love you, Max. Maybe I still do. More than any other man I've ever met. Will you give me time to think about it?"

"How much time? Five minutes, ten?"

"A little more than that." She stood on tiptoe to kiss the tip of his nose. "At least a few days."

He didn't want to wait a few days. Desire and low cunning overcame his scruples and all his resolutions to exercise restraint. Deciding to use every weapon at his disposal he gathered her into his arms again and took a long, delicious kiss that left them both shaky and breathless.

"Give me your answer tomorrow," he said with a gasp.

"No, but I'll take another kiss."

"Come to my bedchamber and I'll do even better."

She was considering it, he could tell. His groin ached at the thought of Eleanor naked between linen sheets, of taking her now, and not letting her go until she was thoroughly pleasured, totally compromised, and possibly pregnant to boot.

With regret and a measure of relief he watched her slowly shake her head. "It's just as well," he said. "I want you to come to me freely, without a shadow of doubt or coercion. You are worth waiting for."

A dazzling smile was his reward. "Thank you, Max. I'm tempted by your offer, but I don't want to risk getting with child. I only returned your letters when I knew I had not conceived. It would have been dreadful to be forced to wed you for such a reason. I suppose we'd better return before we create a scandal."

He wasn't ready to let her go. "I'd like to show you something. Beyond that topiary there's a border planted with all white flowers. They look their best by moonlight."

"How charming. I'd like to see that."

"There's a little summerhouse from which one can sit and view it. It has a very comfortable bench."

In all her sensible days, Eleanor had never received such a romantic offer as a comfortable bench away from prying eyes and the scent of summer flowers in the night. Turning down Max's suggestion of a bed had taken all her willpower. A wellspring of joy in her breast made her want to say yes to all and anything Max proposed, including a hasty marriage. But a lifetime's habit of caution told her to wait. A decision to abandon her devoutly held beliefs must be made in the cold light of day.

There was no reason she couldn't indulge herself a little more. She could enjoy a goodnight kiss. "Lead on," she said. "I expect you to tell me the names of all the flowers."

He snatched a quick taste of her lips and hurried her, their fingers enlaced, into the forest of carved box topiary figures. For a minute or two, she was blind, aware only of Max's large, rough hand guiding her, inspiring her trust. So dark was the walk, that emerging into the open dazed her for a moment. The scent of roses assaulted her nostrils and she looked about her to get her bearings. In the moonlight, she took in the promised summerhouse, a pretty faux-rustic structure of moss-covered stone.

From Max's muttered oath she knew he saw him at the same time as she did, a man, leaving the little building, looking about him carefully. They melted back into the shadows until Robert Townsend had taken the direct route toward the house.

"What's the boy up to . . ."

His sentence was left unfinished at the emergence of another figure, wearing a familiar white gown. Eleanor's instinct was to race forward and confront Caro, but Max's arm restrained her and a minute's reflection convinced her that discretion was the better course.

"Oh dear," was all she could think of to say once the girl had left.

"I'm sorry," Max said.

"It's not your fault. Let's hope things haven't gone too far."

"If they have, I shall make sure Robert marries her. I won't allow Miss Brotherton to be ruined."

"What kind of solution would that be?" Eleanor demanded. "Married at the age of seventeen, to a wild youth of dubious character? What chance of happiness would she have?"

That Eleanor slept at all that night was a miracle. Lying awake for what felt like hours, unable to find a comfortable spot in her bed, she relived the evening. Max's revelation of Sir George Ashdown's role in the fiasco had extinguished the last vestige of anger over the bet. But now she had to face a far more frightening decision. Drowning in the memory of his kisses, the answer seemed obvious. Why not seize a lifetime of such delights? Yet as Eleanor rolled her neck on a pillow that had become lumpy since last night, her stomach lurched with raw fear. Awaking, thirsty and unrefreshed, she prayed Max wouldn't call today. She needed far more time before relinquishing the principles of a lifetime.

It was later than her usual hour of rising, but still early for the morning after a ball. She'd wager Caro wouldn't be up for hours. She rang for her maid, took a greedy drink, and washed in cold water. By the time she had dressed she felt as restless as ever. The day seemed unbearably hot.

Flinging up the sash window that overlooked the front of the house, she saw a horseman ride up. No one had a better seat than Max. Her heart skipped ten beats and her mouth became dry again. As he dismounted and handed the reins to a servant, he looked over the façade of the house, as though searching for something. For her. Even from two floors up she could see his kind, rugged face, imagine the twinkle in his eyes. Damn him! Why couldn't he have waited another day, or three. She might very well tear downstairs and cast herself into his arms. She stumbled back from the window and collapsed into a chair, twisting her hands together.

Five minutes later a servant knocked. "There's a gentleman to see you, Miss Hardwick."

"Tell him I'm still in bed. I won't be receiving callers today."

When the door handle rattled again she panicked. "No," she called. "I'm not dressed."

"Yes you are!" Caro said as she came in, still in her nightgown. "Why did you say you weren't? Oh never mind. Wasn't that the most wonderful evening?"

Eleanor grasped at the distraction. Scolding Caro for last night's behavior gave her a practical task.

"What can you have been thinking of?" she demanded. "Going alone to the summerhouse with Robert Townsend was a terrible indiscretion."

"Don't be a stuffy old thing, Eleanor," Caro said with a pout. "I want to talk about the ball. Wasn't it wonderful?" She clambered up onto the bed and bounced on her knees in an ecstasy of delight. Just the reaction a young girl should have after her first ball. She looked innocent and fragile and Eleanor's heart swelled with a fierce protective love.

"If your mother finds out, she'll never let you visit me. In fact, she'll very likely refuse to take you to London next spring."

"I don't care. I don't want a London season with Mama. Robert says *ton* events are dreadfully dull. He and his friends never go to them. They know much better ways to amuse themselves."

"That may be true, but your only choices are *ton* parties in London, or staying home in Somerset. Which of those two is more *dreadfully dull*?" Eleanor leaned over and took the girl's hand. "Caro, my sweet, I'm glad you've had the chance to meet some young men this summer, and get out of the house. In my opinion your mother is much too particular, but she's not entirely wrong. Virtue is not enough. You must be careful not to let people believe you unchaste. Disappearing at a ball with a young man is just the kind of thing that gives a young girl a bad reputation. If that happens you will never have the chance to wed, whether you wish to or not."

"Of course I will." Caro spoke with utter conviction. "I'm going to marry Robert."

"Has he offered for you?"

"Not yet. But he will. He loves me."

Eleanor sighed. At a naïve seventeen, Caro trod a rocky path. Then she remembered. Townsend was leaving the county immediately. Instead of arguing the girl out of marriage, Eleanor should prepare her for heartbreak. It was all for the best, but she didn't relish the task. She had no stomach for difficult encounters today.

Caro, who was giddy but not stupid, interrupted her dithering thoughts. "How did you know we were in the summerhouse? We were careful not to be seen." The question struck Eleanor silent, but Caro had her own answer. "I suppose you were walking in the garden with Mr. Quinton."

"Why would I do that?"

"Because he fancies you. I think you may fancy him, too. But I *know* he wants you. And Robert has been helping him."

"What?"

"How do you think he always knows where you'll be, and when? Because I tell Robert and Robert tells him."

"But—" Eleanor's mind reeled. She'd suspected, of course, and Max had virtually confirmed that he made a point of tracing her movements. But that Robert and *Caro* were in the conspiracy. "How did this come about? Does Mr. Quinton know Robert gets the intelligence from you?"

"I should think he must, since he told Robert to do it. Robert liked me when he first saw me. When we fell into the river. But he didn't think much of it until Max—Mr. Quinton—suggested he get to know me better since I seemed a pretty girl. But Robert knew straightaway that it was you Mr. Quinton was interested in. We've had great fun, sending messages back and forth and making plans for you and Mr. Quinton to meet."

Eleanor felt dizzy as she watched Caro, so blithe and happy and completely unaware of the effect of her words which seemed to come from a great distance. "I'm so glad it happened, because otherwise Robert wouldn't have fallen in love with me."

How could he be so callous? Caro was going to be miserable and it was all Max's fault.

CHAPTER FIVE

Lancashire

"Oh! you're here, my dear. When did you arrive?"

Eleanor dropped a kiss on her father's gray head. "Last night, Papa." There was no point in reminding Mr. Hardwick that he'd greeted her when she arrived late last evening, finding him deep in a book.

The same book, a hefty leather-bound tome, had been brought to the breakfast room. The Reverend Thomas Hardwick didn't let the mundane requirements of the body keep him from his studies.

Or conversation.

As he consulted the index and flipped to the desired page, Eleanor helped herself to bread and butter and poured herself a cup of tea.

"Pass the marmalade, please Papa."

Blinking like an owl, Mr. Hardwick looked around the table in vain.

"At your elbow. Careful you don't get it on the pages."

Finding and passing the dish of preserves seemed to awake

him from his scholarly haze. "Did you have a good journey from Derbyshire?" he asked. "How was Cuthbert?"

"Cousin Cuthbert lives in Kent," she replied calmly. "I was in Somerset with the Brothertons. Mama's cousin Elizabeth, and Caro."

"Ah yes. The little girl. She must be nine or ten by now." Caro had, miraculously, managed to make an impression on Mr. Hardwick, who rarely remembered anyone who wasn't interested in the natural history of the Bible. During a brief visit years earlier, she had attempted to lift a rare edition of Culpepper's Herbal and dropped it on her five-year-old toes. Luckily the book had sustained no more permanent damage than did the child.

"I hope her foot recovered."

"She is seventeen and walks without a discernible limp."

"I'm glad to hear it. Did you enjoy your visit? Not too hot in the West Country?"

Eleanor didn't want to talk about it. Neither did her father. "Is that Stackhouse's *History of the Bible?*" she asked. "I should think you know it by heart."

"I've been comparing what he has to say with Pilkington's essay on the Mount of Olives and a new explanation came to me last night. I must write to Dr. Farrell at Cambridge. He will be most interested."

Listening to her father ramble on about his obsession was balm to Eleanor's soul after the storm of the past weeks. Buffeted by the uncertain yearnings of her heart and the undeniable rage of physical desire, she found rest in her father's almost indifferent affection. He loved her, of course, but he didn't need her. He made no demands beyond a sympathetic ear. Life could return to normal, to the enjoyment of cool reason, free from the upheavals that Max Quinton had twice wrought on her unwilling emotions. In the dining room of her lifelong home, with the cold mist of a Lancashire summer polishing the varied greens of the shrubbery near the open window, she felt at peace.

During the long journey home she had raged at Max's manipulative deception. That he would jeopardize the happiness of an innocent girl to get close to her again demonstrated the same careless indifference with which he'd entered a contest to crack the guarded heart of a spinster, and then robbed the pitiful old maid of her virtue.

That the spinster in no way regarded herself as pitiful and in fact reveled in her old-maidhood was irrelevant. Max and his cronies had regarded her as a dried-up prune in need of softening up. But now she was home and ready to forget the whole sorry business. Again. She thought she'd forgiven him, but her anger had returned in greater force. Panic about disrupting the calm of her rational existence had nothing to do with it. It was anger that had driven her away, not fear.

Mr. Hardwick, whose soft discourse had faded from her consciousness, stared in surprise as she slammed her cup down, breaking one of her mother's Worcester saucers into two neat halves. "I beg your pardon, Papa. I slipped."

Yes, she had slipped. Twice. Slipped into a crevasse and broken an entire dinner service. Her brief respite of serenity was over. The room was too hot, despite a mild summer drizzle outside the open window. The lace trim of her gown scratched her neck. Her scalp felt itchy.

"I must see Mrs. Hibbert. Perhaps she can mend this."

Mrs. Hibbert could. The housekeeper went over the accounts with Eleanor and consulted her on a couple of minor problems that she could have easily solved on her own. The staff was quite adequate to the task of caring for the comfortable parsonage and its eccentric master.

These banal tasks restored Eleanor to a state of serenity bordering on somnolence. Being at home always did. Wistfully she thought of the busy life she'd left behind in Somerset: friendly neighbors and an agreeable social circle. What her Lancashire life had always lacked. Mr. Hardwick's living was not a prosperous one, neither was his parish busy. He liked it that way, had indeed accepted the position because it asked so little of him and allowed him ample time to study. The county was traditionally Catholic and the neighborhood gentry and their tenants adhered to Rome, holding themselves aloof from the representatives of the established Church. They required little pastoral care and offered no society. Like her mother before her, Eleanor was bored to distraction.

The distraction she sought in visits to her numerous relations, where she could participate in the pursuits of the gentlewoman. How much happier would her lively mother have been had she been an active vicar's wife, like Mrs. Walpole, busy with friends, a growing family, and her husband's advancement. Instead she had supercilious Catholics and a spouse who needed no help, unless he happened to have mislaid a rare pamphlet on the origins of barley. And a child, just one, a well-behaved and self-sufficient little girl. Had Eleanor been as much of a hoyden as Caro, perhaps her mother would have felt needed and stayed alive.

Poor Mama. She hadn't the option of travel, as Eleanor had. She couldn't take off for balls and horse races and enjoyable interference in the lives of her erring relatives. She'd been a married woman and tied to her husband.

If Eleanor wasn't to go mad with no one but her lovable and oblivious father to keep her from brooding on Max Quinton, she'd better find another cousin who needed some bracing advice. In her current mood, she'd even consider the Ashdowns. She'd take a good deal of pleasure in making life miserable for Sir George.

The next day, she eagerly shuffled through the post, hoping for a summons from another county. Surely all her relations hadn't been simultaneously struck down with health, happiness, and the pursuit of common sense? There had to be an only son who wanted to join the army, a mother of four with a broken leg, or a daughter with a broken heart.

There was but one missive inscribed with her name, in Caro's unorthodox penmanship. Poor child! Her only qualm about her rapid departure from Sedgehill had been leaving Caro before she learned of Robert's inconstancy. She'd done her best to prepare the way, persuading Cousin Elizabeth to let Caro accompany the Markhams to Bath for a week or two.

"Robert will find me there," Caro had whispered happily.

Eleanor left her illusions intact. The likelihood of Robert Townsend abandoning the delights of London for starchy Bath seemed less than nothing. By that time, she trusted, the pangs of first love would have diminished.

She took her time opening the letter, fetching a knife to slice under the seal with a good deal more care than its sender had used in its application, judging by the splash of red wax on the

folded sheet. A quick survey told her that Caro didn't mention
Max Quinton. Perhaps he hadn't even called at Sedgehill. Perhaps he'd taken her request for a few days reflection seriously.
Or maybe he'd thought better of his proposal. Which was fine
and proved Eleanor had made the right decision. Again.

> Dearest Eleanor,
>   I wish you hadn't left in such a hurry because you've
> missed such goings-on. I want you to be the first to know that
> I am to be married! I told you so, and you wouldn't believe it.
> But right after you left, my darling Robert spoke to Mama.

Eleanor's heart sank. She would have expected Elizabeth
Brotherton to forbid the match, not because Robert was
young and wild but because he didn't have the high title she
craved for her daughter.

> She said no, of course. I knew she would. Mama never
> lets me do what I want and she doesn't like Robert because
> he isn't a horrid old marquess. I told Robert not to even
> bother asking for her permission but he said he might as well
> do the right thing for once. Mama said I'd shown I was too
> young to be out so I was going to have to come back in again
> until next year. No trip to Bath and no more evening parties
> till we go to London. So we leave tonight for Gretna Green.

Cousin Elizabeth hadn't disappointed after all. She'd be-
haved with predictable narrow-minded stupidity and driven
Caro to rebellion. With rising dismay Eleanor read her way
through an account of the juvenile couple's elopement plans

to the sorry conclusion that proved Caro's lack of readiness for marriage.

> By the time you read this, I daresay I shall be married and should sign myself
> Caroline Townsend.
>
> P.S. Finally I'm leaving Somerset.
> P.P.S. I'm so happy!
> P.P.P.S. Love is <u>delicious</u>. You should try it.

Eleanor tore upstairs and started packing. A decade of visiting all over England had given her an extensive knowledge of roads, distances, and travel arrangements, and a much better grasp of timing than Robert Townsend and his feckless friends. According to Caro, she and the four young men would travel first to Lord Kendal's family estate to borrow a carriage. Eleanor had cast her eyes to the ceiling when she read that Robert lacked sufficient ready money to travel post all the way to Scotland. There was little chance they would arrive at the border for another two days. When they did, Eleanor intended to be there, to prevent this most disastrous of matches.

"Off already, my dear?" was all Mr. Hardwick had to say when she went to his study, garbed for the road.

"Caro needs me."

"The little girl? Did her foot get worse?"

Explanation was futile. "I shall take the carriage to the Red Lion and engage a post chaise. I'll write and let you know when to expect me home."

Unlike Robert Townsend, Eleanor always had a supply

of guineas in the house, ready for a journey. Sixty-odd miles by post would be expensive and curtail the purchases she'd planned for her London wardrobe. Caro's future was worth the loss of a gown or two.

She entered the Red Lion Inn, where she was a frequent and well-respected customer. "Good morning, Clitheroe. I need a carriage. I'm going to visit my cousin near Carlisle." No need to mention Gretna and give rise to undesirable speculation. And no need to explain the absence of a traveling companion. Her own standing in the county, her frequent travel, and advanced age should be enough to quell impertinent questions.

"I'm sorry Miss Hardwick. You should have sent word," the landlord replied. "This gentleman just engaged the last one."

She hadn't even noticed the large figure lingering in the shadowy hall. "Good morning, Miss Hardwick. Fancy meeting you here."

She almost betrayed herself into expressing the moment's joy she felt at seeing his reassuringly large figure. He'd come after her! "Mr. Quinton. What a surprise."

His expression conveyed no reciprocating pleasure. She'd never seen Max so grim.

"You know this gentleman?" Clitheroe asked. "Happen he's headed for Carlisle, too. Pity you couldn't share the carriage but it wouldn't be fit, what with you being alone without your maid."

"Certainly not." So he hadn't come to find her. In fact he must be on the same mission as she.

"If you're concerned with propriety," he said curtly, "I can take you as far as the next change where you can hire your own chaise."

Clitheroe nodded at the happy solution and Eleanor had to admit it made sense. "Very well, Mr. Quinton. I accept your offer. I'm sure I can hire my own carriage at Burton."

The advantage of speed when traveling post was balanced by the cramped quarters offered by the light carriage. Especially when one had to share it with a large man with whom one was scarcely on speaking terms.

She was the first to break a charged silence. "I take it we are on the same mission."

"Why else would I have undertaken a two-hundred-mile journey?" His voice was flat and brisk, quite unlike his usual amiable tone.

"Robert Townsend is no longer your ward."

"I still feel a responsibility."

"So you should. Caro told me she and Robert kept you informed of our plans so you could get close to me. You used a pair of foolish children, as you quite rightly called them."

"I wondered if that was the reason you left Somerset without even doing me the courtesy of responding to my proposal. Last time, at least, I was not abandoned without explanation."

She was on treacherous ground here, and she knew it, so she attacked. "As a result of your callous manipulation, my poor little cousin will be trapped into a terrible marriage and her reputation ruined. And it's *your* fault."

"And I accept my share of responsibility. Had I paid more attention, I would have noticed things between them had progressed so far." He regarded her steadily and she refused to meet his eye, staring forward at the fustian wall of the chaise. His attention had been on her. Hers had been equally absent from her cousin and she felt her failure deeply.

"However," he continued, "Robert offered for Miss Brotherton. He told me he would when I scolded him after the ball. I came to tell you the next morning but you were still abed. When the pair of us called the day after, you had left."

Squeezing her eyes shut, Eleanor absorbed the fact that she might have saved her cousin. "Oh Lord. And now she is ruined."

"If she's ruined, her mother must share the blame. They are both young, it is true, but Robert is of good birth and has a healthy fortune, as I am in a position to know. Not only did she turn him down flat, she refused to let him see Caro again. Her intransigence precipitated the elopement."

"My cousin acted stupidly, I agree. She should have postponed the engagement but let them continue to see each other. Very likely the infatuation would have run its course."

"Exactly! We think alike. We can only hope for things to go well with them. It's true I took advantage of the information Robert learned from Caro." His voice dropped. "You can blame me for the deception, but I was a man in love."

"You ordered him to court her! Do you know how soiled it makes me feel that I was in any part responsible for their coming together? I thought I could forgive the sordidness of your wager. But this. It is too much."

"You misunderstand the matter. That had nothing to do with you. I suggested Robert cultivate Miss Brotherton's company because I thought an innocent flirtation a more wholesome occupation for him than losing his fortune at cards."

"Oh!" she shrieked. "So he is a gamester! My poor Caro!"

"No! Not a gamester. At least I hope not. And surely not irredeemable. Perhaps marriage will steady him."

Eleanor snorted. "If I have anything to say about it we'll never find out. I intend to save her. I shall find her and take her home. We'll tell everyone she was with me all the time."

"I'm afraid that won't work. Her mother and brother have already disowned her."

"The devil they have!" It took a lot to make Eleanor utter a profanity.

"I went to Mrs. Brotherton to discuss what should best be done. Good God, Eleanor! What a foolish and disagreeable woman she is. She fed me some nonsense about wishing her daughter to marry Kendal or a marquess, and told me that under no circumstances would she ever speak to her daughter again. I soon found she'd made not the least effort to hush the business up and the news was already spread around the neighborhood."

"If only I had been there! I could have reasoned with her."

"Why weren't you?" he asked. "Why did you leave?"

"I—" She paused. "You know why. I don't wish to speak of it. We must decide what to do about the children."

Max's ears strained to hear her words. She'd started to say something different and changed her mind. Something important. His bewildered anger at her fickleness had haunted the long journey into Lancashire. Yet he'd have sworn on any ancestral grave anyone cared to produce that Eleanor was not capricious. Her affections to all but him were unchangeable. And her flight had been irrational.

A tinge of dark humor tugged the edge of his mouth when

he considered her probable reaction to such an accusation. He loved her for her much vaunted common sense, of which commodity she'd shown precious little in her dealings with him. The human heart rarely traded in logic. An acorn of hope sprouted in his breast. Lips pursed, eyes straight ahead, she was not to be argued with . . . yet.

"Let us agree that we are neither without fault and try to make the best of the situation." He spoke dispassionately and resisted a strong desire to take her hand, to comfort her distress if nothing more. "Her only choice is to marry Robert. And since it's what she wants, what they both want, it could be worse. If I, Robert's former guardian, and you, representing Caro's family, are present for the wedding, perhaps we can salvage things enough that they will be received. That *she* will be received. You are conversant enough with the way things are to know that it is always the lady who pays."

"You are right," she said in a subdued tone. "Caro does need me."

Riding in silence for several miles, Max took quiet satisfaction each time a bump in the road marred the unyielding line of Eleanor's back and lurched her to his side of the bench. Every brush of her shoulder gave him promise for the future. He was prepared to take one stage of their journey at a time. He and his infuriated beloved were speeding for Gretna Green, and not to take advantage of the place's famous facilities would be a travesty. One particularly sharp jolt almost knocked her off the seat. The hand she extended to save herself landed on his thigh, inches from causing him extreme pain. "You'll pay for that, my love," he murmured, too low for her to make out the words. She glared at him, resumed her rigid posture, and stuck her nose into the air without uttering a word.

Thus she remained when they pulled into the innyard at Burton. "Stay here," he said, opening the door. "I'll inquire about hiring another carriage for you."

A few words, a couple of coins, and a promise of further largesse, and the change was made at record speed. In the past, he'd made the mistake of accepting her refusal. Never again. He had Eleanor where he wanted her and he intended to keep her there until she agreed to marry him. He returned to the carriage and closed the door as the post boy whipped up the leader and they trotted smartly out into the road.

"Stop!" The single word broke almost half an hour's silence.

"I've decided there's no point traveling in two vehicles," he said. "It wouldn't be thrifty."

"You have no right to make such a decision. How I spend my money is my own affair."

"That I don't dispute. But when our destination and our goal is the same it seems foolish not to join forces."

"I'm getting out at the next inn," she said.

"You may do as you wish. But the post boy says there's no likelihood of finding another vehicle for hire before Penrith."

Her irritated sniff told him his information was correct. "I cannot stay at an inn in your company! The innkeeper will think we are eloping."

No need to mention that the post boys already thought so. "If we make good time there's no reason we shouldn't reach the border tonight. Then we can stay in different inns."

For the first time since they'd met at the inn, she smiled.

"Are you familiar with this part of the country?" He made a noncommittal noise. He hadn't spent much time in the north. "More familiar with East Anglia, I think?" she said.

"I have a map."

"Very flat was how you described your home," Eleanor said. "Well it does not describe the terrain between here and Carlisle. We'll be lucky to make it by tomorrow evening, and only if it doesn't rain and turn the roads to mud."

"Damn," he cursed. "I beg your pardon, but I hoped I had overtaken Robert. I lost track of him in Somerset and don't know which road they took."

She explained about Robert's plans as detailed in Caro's letter, drawing an incredulous shake of Max's head. "I suppose," she said, her voice tinged with amusement, "he couldn't ask you for advice about how to obtain the money to elope. I hope his ability to read a map is better than yours. The Red Lion Inn was quite out of your way."

"I came to find you. I was on my way to call on you at home."

"Why?"

"Aside from wishing to discover why the lady I'd proposed to had traveled half the length of England without giving me an answer? I came to tell you about the elopement."

"There was no need, as you know."

"I told you my plan to restore her respectability. She needs your help."

"She needs my help not getting married. I shall lend her countenance, claim I have been with her all along."

He gave up the argument and set his mind to another problem. He had fifty miles to discover why Eleanor was so set against marriage and to change her mind.

"The road seems in excellent condition."

"Lucky," she said, replying to his opening for the first time in a couple of hours. "It seems the weather has been unusually dry." It was annoying to be proven wrong, but at least she'd reach Penrith and the safety of her own carriage that much sooner. Being cooped up in close quarters with Max was addling her mind. She wasn't sure how much longer she could take it. The farther they went, the less she remembered exactly why she was so angry at him.

"I don't believe," she continued, "they can be ahead of us, but there's a chance we will reach Carlisle tonight. They have to pass through the town and it shouldn't be hard to get word of them if they've already been there."

"Don't worry, my dear," he said. "Even if we are too late for the wedding, we can still save Caro's reputation."

He thought Caro should be married and there was no point arguing. It was safer to remain silent. She had her plans laid for escaping him and reaching Scotland first. The alternative was too dreadful. She squeezed back a tear.

"Are you crying?" His large hand covered hers, clenched together in her lap. "It'll be all right. We'll make it so, I promise."

Her unwilling heart responded to the kindness of his tone. He was a good man, despite his errors. She didn't agree with him, but his faults were of carelessness, not malice.

"You should have children, Eleanor," he said. "I've seen you with Caro, and with young people of different ages. You will be a wonderful mother."

The devil. He'd found her weakness. Though she tried

not to admit it to herself, there had been a seed of regret that she hadn't been with child after their union. Regret quickly smothered with relief because she wouldn't have to marry him.

"I am content with the company of other people's offspring for I shall never marry." She was uneasily aware that she sought to convince herself, as well as him.

"Because of me? Because of what happened between us?" Anguish lay beneath his gentle tone. It had never occurred to her that he'd also been hurt. Yet if what he'd told her about the wager and Ashdown was true—and she believed it was—he deserved some kind of explanation.

She shook her head, then met his gaze with as much calm as she could muster. "What happened five years ago was an aberration on my part. For a few days you made me forget a lifetime's resolution. Long observation has taught me that marriages rarely turn out well."

"That's ridiculous. I know many happily married men and women."

"And I know many who are unhappily married."

"I grant you there are no certainties, but the odds seem good. Better than even, I would venture to say. And think of the rewards, the great happiness a loving partnership can bring."

"And think of the misery of a poor one. Think of Sylvia and Ashdown."

"Not all husbands are oafs."

"No. Wives can inflict unhappiness too. Think of my Cousin Elizabeth, who made two husbands miserable."

"Think of Mr. Walpole and his loving wife who shares his concerns and warms his bed."

She blushed, remembering his subtle paean to the marriage bed in Mrs. Markham's drawing room. If only the marriage bed was all there was to it. But he'd spoken of a marriage of true minds that day.

She shook off his hand and the dangerously attractive notion of marriage to him. "The chance of grief is too great to be worth the risk. Take my own parents. I don't know why they wed, for they had nothing in common. I believe my father wished for someone to keep house for him so he wouldn't be troubled with practicalities while he pursued his studies. My mother was a sweet, warm creature, fond of conversation and company. She withered away under his neglect."

"She had you."

Her mouth pinched in distress. "The company of a little girl wasn't enough to make up for the lack of affection from her spouse."

"How old were you when she died?"

"Ten."

"Poor lonely little girl. No wonder you spend your time traveling, looking for companionship."

"Don't pity me," she said fiercely. "I am the most fortunate of women. My fortune is sufficient for my needs and no husband tells me how to spend it, or squanders it on horseflesh or the gaming tables. No one tells me where I may go or with whom I may speak or complains when I buy a new hat."

"I do not squander my money and I make a good income from horseflesh," he replied. She knew that, and even admired his knowledge and hard work. "I can safely promise I would never object to your millinery. I find it absurd and delightful in equal parts."

"*Men are April when they woo, December when they wed.* You see, Mr. Quinton, I can quote Shakespeare too. And I have had many occasions to observe the truth of those words."

"The Bard of Avon has a phrase for every occasion. *The lady doth protest too much, methinks.*" His voice sank to a caress and she could feel his breath on her cheek. "Don't you wish for a family and a home of your own, instead of living through the trials of others? That's what I offer. I make no guarantee, but you can be assured of my love."

He slid his arm around her shoulders and she stiffened her spine as longing flooded her veins, fighting the wild instinct of flight. "Eleanor," he whispered. Her name was a siren call, buzzing in her ear. The chaise was slowing down and a glance through the window told her they were coming into Penrith. She need only be strong for a few more minutes. "My love."

Her idiot body betrayed her. Her breasts swelled, remembering the one time they'd enjoyed the touch of a man's hand. Heat bloomed in the core he'd once filled. Because it could be for only a minute, she surrendered to temptation and turned to meet the rock of his chest. They melted into each other and she knew he shared her weakness. But the advantage was hers for she also knew it was for only a minute and she put all her desire and regret into a kiss that would be their last. She tried to imprint the texture and taste of him on her memory so she could take it with her. When the chaise jolted to a halt, she was ready to run for her life.

Chapter Six

Like Samson betrayed by lust, Max watched his Delilah disappear into the inn. But he still had his hair, and he recovered philosophically from his defeat. Whatever she claimed, she wanted him and he wouldn't let her escape. He understood her now. Let her waste her money, which would be better spent on the personal adornment that he fully intended would be worn in the future for his own pleasure. He'd let her play it her way for a while. They still had a couple of hours of daylight and he knew where she was going. Carlisle was only twenty miles on. Flee him as she might, his pursuit was steadfast and wily.

Inside he found her negotiating with the innkeeper. He passed her with a nod and proceeded to the taproom to order a bite to eat for the road. Emerging refreshed to the innyard he learned his clever darling had outwitted him. She was climbing into a chaise harnessed with four horses—at an additional cost of at least two expensive bonnets. She gave him a triumphant wave as the equipage trotted smartly into the road and he tipped his hat to her with a grin. Without a companion or much baggage, he could travel on horseback and if there was one thing Max did well it was ride.

It was a decent nag, though not up to his standards. At the ten-mile change he was only a few minutes behind her. His new mount was slower, but he sensed excellent stamina that would keep pace all the way to their destination. About five miles on he spotted a splash of yellow that could only be a post chaise up ahead at the side of the road.

"Do you need help?" he asked. The postillion assured him the broken trace could be mended in little time. Having examined the harness himself he saw that it was true. The man seemed competent, so there was no danger that Eleanor would be left on the road all night. Nevertheless, it would be ungentlemanly not to offer.

"Shall I take you up before me?" he asked her.

Her response was a scowling and emphatic negative. Whistling merrily, he rode on with a new plan in mind.

With the patched-up trace, they had to take the rest of the journey slowly. Eleanor kept telling herself she must be well ahead of the eloping couple. She could spend the night at Carlisle and hire someone to take her to the Scottish border in the morning to intercept Caro. But mostly she tried, and failed, not to think about that unwise kiss. How was she to face Max Quinton again?

Alas for her desperate hope that Max, being on horseback, would have chosen a different inn. He was waiting in the entrance hall.

"Here she is," he said, before she had a chance to speak to

the innkeeper. "What kept you, my dear? I was concerned." Her rumbling stomach fought the instinct to dash out before the horses were unhitched. "You must be hungry and tired but don't worry. I have ordered a fine supper in our rooms, then you can seek your bed." Before she could utter a snappish refusal he turned to the waiting host. "My wife is travel worn. Pray have hot water sent up immediately. Come, Eleanor. I will show you the way."

He was devilishly clever. She couldn't proclaim her true identity without causing a scandal. If she gave a false name and denied him, there would be a most unpleasant scene. She let him remove her valise from her nerveless grasp. In her state of starvation she'd let him feed her, but only the fact that he'd inserted the pronoun *your* before the word *bed* saved him from imminent murder. She summoned enough strength to dig her nails into his offered arm and hoped it hurt through the broadcloth of his sleeve.

The presence of servants kept her from responding to his string of soothing platitudes on the way upstairs to a pleasant parlor, then she had to suffer having her linen jacket tenderly removed, her fichu straightened. He even took off her high crowned hat for her.

"I don't believe I've seen this one before. Is it new? Very fetching. You must buy more in different colors." Since the oversized bow decorating the crown had got in his way when they kissed in the close quarters of the post chaise, only extreme annoyance kept her from smiling. Instead she broke away, followed a maid with a can of hot water into the adjoining chamber, and slammed the door.

She grudgingly admitted it was agreeable not to have to

wait for a room. Clearly this was one of the best in the house, possessing its own water closet and handsome furniture. But how Max spent his money was no business of hers. She was *not* his wife and she had every intention of occupying that large bed alone. Washed and refreshed, she pursued enticing smells back to the parlor where servants were laying out a repast.

"What are you doing?" she whispered beneath the clatter of dishes.

"Demonstrating the benefits of having a husband," he said, and kissed her neck as he pushed in her chair.

There was a dreamlike quality to the meal, sitting across from Max, being served delicious food and good wine by well-trained attendants. He kept up a flow of talk to which she had to respond or look petty. Cleverly, he described a visit to a horse-loving peer. He spoke as though they'd been apart for some weeks and he was filling her in on his news. She found it alluring to listen to his concerns and successes, to hear of the pride and pleasure he took in his affairs. Dangerously alluring.

She ate half a dish of syllabub and felt warm, contented, and well fed. Silence fell, thick with unspoken wishes. The clatter of her spoon on the saucer cracked like a gunshot. She fixed her attention on the melting pudding because it was perilous to look up and meet the heated gaze she sensed on her downcast face. The presence of the bed next door loomed large. The servants were clearing the table. Soon they would be alone. She felt soft and weak.

The last servant closed the door behind him.

"So, Mrs. Q.," he said, stretching across the table to take

her hand. His was warm and large and shot heat through her. Her heart flipped over. "Are you ready for bed?"

Thank God he'd given her reason to object.

"Are you mad?" she sputtered, snatching away her hand and thrusting back her chair.

"I thought perhaps you are tired and need rest." Outraged innocence was belied by the laughter in his slumberous eyes. "What else did you think I meant? Unless invited to share the bed, I shall sleep in here."

She wanted to invite him. "I only went along with this farce because our object in coming to this place is to prevent a scandal, not to cause one." She retreated to the cold hearth "What we should do now is call on every inn in town and find out if Caro and Robert are here."

He followed her and she deflected his advance with the flat of her hand.

"Be calm, my angel. I took care of it when I arrived in the town. And distributed a little bribery at each place. We'll be informed if they appear. Most likely it will be tomorrow and we can hire a vehicle to follow them north and attend the wedding."

"Stop the wedding, you mean."

"No," he said firmly. "The marriage must take place. There is no alternative. They've been traveling together for several days. Caro is ruined."

"Perhaps not."

"You know that's an absurd statement. Besides, I've been thinking. Did you never wonder how he knew about your blackberrying expedition, which had been agreed upon only the night before? Is it possible the little minx had been creeping out of the house at night to meet him?"

Eleanor groaned, remembering a couple of nights when lying awake unable to sleep, thinking about Max—another notch to add to his tally—she'd fancied she had heard someone creeping down the passage. "It's possible." Entirely possible. She'd been blind.

He swept his hair back from his forehead. "I'm sorry this happened and I wish I hadn't encouraged their flirtation. What were we supposed to do? Lock them in their rooms at night?"

She could no longer summon fury at Max. Her indignation had been an excuse to run from him. Just as she'd run from him before. How much longer could she resist him?

Desperately, she rallied again. "And you want her to be tied for life to her debaucher?"

"Now you are being overdramatic. I don't excuse Robert's behavior, but he didn't ravish the girl. We keep calling them children, but they are both old enough to know better. Despite his faults, Robert is a gentleman and intends to marry her." He came closer and met her eye. "That's what gentlemen do," he said sternly.

She looked away. "How very condescending of him! It's unfair that a single so-called slip of virtue should affect her whole life. Why does it have to be thus for women? I reject the idea."

"I am very well aware of that fact. Perhaps it's not fair, but just because you have a head full of bees on the subject doesn't mean there's no such thing as a happy marriage." She shook her head, unable to find an argument. "Robert and Caro have as good a chance as any couple. Better, in fact. Robert wants to marry her. He's in love with her, as she is with him. And if they don't marry, what will she do? Her mother won't take her back."

A fair question and a good argument. "I will look after her," she cried in a final burst of defiance. "She shall come and live with me. We'll take a house in London. Caro will love that."

"My darling! You're deluding yourself. You think you want to save your cousin from marriage," he said relentlessly, "but it's yourself you think to save. If you love Caro, and I know you do, you don't want to condemn her to a narrow life in a pokey London house, shunned by those of her own class and thrown back on the company of her elderly cousin."

He was right, damn him! She never cried, but tears started to pour down her face. "I would not take a pokey house. And I'm not elderly."

His arms surrounded her and she was pulled against the sanctuary of his chest. "You're in the prime of life, my darling. And you need to stop taking care of other people's children and have some of your own."

She sobbed into his neckcloth and let herself surrender to the comfort of his murmured endearments. He stroked her back and told her he loved her and years of denial melted away. As her tears subsided to snuffles, the superb fact of being in Max's arms with a large bed a room a way seeped into her mind. And apparently his too. He swept her up, with no more effort than if she were a doll, and made for the bedroom door.

"Er . . . " Her protest was for form only, not even expressed in a single English word. She'd had enough of saying no.

"Quiet," he said, "or I'll tie you up." And deposited her on the bed. And landed on top of her.

There was no finesse in his loving assault. She reveled in his weight, in the way his powerful body covered and enclosed her, and the punishing possession of his kiss. She was taken back to the first time she'd been with Max. Ever since she'd been convincing herself she made a massive mistake in giving herself to him. But leaving had been the mistake. Rejecting and missing so many years of his kisses on her lips and neck, of his hands, slightly callused, delving under her garments and finding her aching breasts that swelled and throbbed under his stroking, of his hot mouth sucking on her nipples and sending streaks of bliss down a line that connected to the passage between her thighs.

Were all men as wonderful as this? Did they all give kisses that tasted like the mead of the gods, caresses that made her skin feel like shimmering satin? Of course not! Only Max. That's why she'd spent her youth avoiding them and failed to understand that in him, she'd found something profoundly special.

She pushed on his shoulders and at once he raised his head from her breast, wary consternation on his rough, handsome face. He was breathing heavily. "It's all right," she said. "I wanted to see you, that's all. Last time it was dark."

His smile went straight to her heart. "Good. I was afraid I would have to tie you up after all?"

"Would you really do that?"

He swiveled his hips as they lay between her legs so she felt his hard member against her sex through their layers of clothing. "Not unless you wanted it. I will never do anything you don't want, Eleanor."

"This, from the man who forced me to dine and sleep with him by claiming we were married."

"But I knew you wanted that. At least the dining part."

"It was a very fine dinner."

"And the sleeping will be fine, too. Eventually. I want to see you too. Every inch of you."

Last time, they'd pushed aside their garments in a haphazard fashion, exposing a breast here, a leg there, and the part of each of them that mattered for coupling. This time the undressing was no less frantic but a good deal more thorough. She'd never bared herself to a man's gaze before, but a moment's consideration quieted her fears that he might find her nakedness less than enticing. She'd wasted the firmer flesh of her youth on celibacy and her stomach wasn't as flat or her breasts as pert as they'd been at eighteen. But Max had chased her the length of England and said he wanted her. So she was what he would get, with all the imperfections of her thirty-year-old body. The look in his eyes when she tossed aside her shift reassured her. Smoldering with desire, they scanned her from chin to toe, his mouth parting in an avid grimace.

She returned the examination as he knelt before her, drinking in the muscled thighs, rough with dark hair; lingering at his male member that strained darkly fascinating toward the pit of his navel; noting the carved ridges of his torso that her hands had once sought beneath his shirt as they lay on the Sussex grass; his chest, dark with hair and bearing a small scar that hinted at a tale she would hear in their future; his shoulders, every bit as powerful as they promised beneath his comfortably loose coats; the Adam's apple in the strong column of his neck. Upwards to his face, as transfixed with happiness as her own must be.

"I love you, Max."

"I've waited so long to hear those words." The rasp of his voice attested to his astonishment and his joy.

"Come to me," she said and opened her arms wide.

Naked touching was even better than clothed. Nothing could equal flesh against flesh, his hands over every inch of her skin, her own exploring the contours of her beloved, as though he were a foreign country to be discovered and possessed. She grew heated and wanting beneath his caresses, gasping in counterpoint to his groans of desire. Blunt fingers found the wet folds of her swollen sex and stroked the little peak, her core of pleasure, until she cried out with delicious frustration.

"Max," she said, a little testily. She raised her hips in an urgent demand that was met with a thrust and received with a grateful shudder. He filled her, body and soul. She reveled in every inch of contact and strained for more, her knees tightening around his hips, her legs curling around the rough abrasion of his legs. She'd been insane to run from this bliss, this physical manifestation of their mutual possession. Her head pressed back into the pillow so that she could see his beloved face, greedy and wild, with no trace of his usual calm amusement. With a surge of pure delight, she knew only she could make him thus. She had the delicious power to drive him to madness, just as he could her. She clenched about his male member, slick and hard as it moved inside her, working muscles she barely knew she had to match the rhythm of his entry.

"My love, my own." Sweet words enhanced her gratification, guiding her in a long climb to heights of pleasure she could scarcely bear yet never wanted to end. "Sweetheart," he groaned. "My darling Eleanor." Every endearment sent her higher till she was gasping for breath, tilting her hips beneath him to seek paradise, squeezing her eyes shut as she focused on the place of their joining. A shift in his position and the root of his member found the sensitive nub and she tumbled, shrieking with an agony of joy as her inner passage shook and waves of ecstasy traveled though her limbs. He shouted in triumph at her completion and she opened her eyes, blurred with happy tears to watch his features, savage and beautiful, as he accelerated to his own noisy bliss.

A passing thought had her wonder if there was anyone in the next room and if they could hear, and if so what they thought. She couldn't bring herself to care when he turned onto his back and pulled her into his arms to lie in damp repletion, their breathing fading into the silence of their own particular world.

Eleanor's head lay on his chest, her dark hair a gossamer halo in the flickering candlelight. Max closed his eyes, idly enjoying the firm pliancy of her arm under his tickling fingers.

"Max?"

"Don't move."

She raised her head. "I want to see you. You're smiling."

"That's because I'm happy. I hope you are, too."

"Open your eyes and look. I want to talk."

He groaned and cracked open his lids. She looked happy, but he wasn't taking things for granted yet, even after that stupefying bedding. "Please don't say you won't marry me. I won't tolerate it. You've had your way with me and now you must pay."

She laughed, then her brow creased. "Supposing we don't make each happy. How can we be certain?"

Clearly he wasn't yet allowed to sink into comatose betrothed bliss. He rolled them over to lie face to face on their sides. "We can't be. But I'm a levelheaded and sensible man. I know I love you and I intend to do everything in my very considerable power to keep us in a state of bliss for the rest of our lives. If you let me have a nap for half an hour or so, I could start again tonight." With a distinct glint in her eye she reached under the covers and fluttered her fingers over his lower stomach. "Nothing yet. I'm not as young as I was. But truly, my darling, I don't know what else to say to convince you to marry me."

"I do want to marry you."

"That's more like it." Something told him this wasn't the moment to suggest they get some sleep. "What worries you?" Soothingly he stroked her delightfully rumpled head.

She raised herself onto one elbow, but didn't seem to be contemplating flight. Still, he was ready to catch her if she bolted. "I've been thinking of things I *don't* want to do. I'm not a bluestocking and I don't want to study obscure subjects. I have no wish to travel to other countries where they have bad roads, dirty inns, and revolutions. I don't want to devote my life to good works."

"That's all right, my love. You don't have to do any of those things."

"I don't want to live alone, like my father. I like company and friends and being busy about everyday things. I am interested in the affairs of people I love and I like to help them." She grimaced. "I told you I had a managing disposition."

"I like that about you. What do you want to do?" He hoped she'd say she wanted manage him.

"I'd like to have a home of my own. I like"—she blushed prettily—"doing what we just did. And I like children. I don't know why I never thought of it before, but do you realize what it means?"

His chest swelled. "It sounds to me like you want to be a wife."

"Isn't it odd?"

"The only odd thing is that you never knew it before. But I'm glad of that because you'd have been snapped up years ago by some lucky fellow. I do hope this long overdue road-to-Damascus conversion means you're going to be *my* wife and have *my* children."

"I'm frightened, Max. I could lose them. I could lose you."

He saw the lonely child, mourning her mother, beneath the strong features of the mature woman who worshipped common sense. "Our children will grow up and leave us, as they should. But I'll still be there."

"You might die." He had to strain to catch the choked words.

"I probably will, eventually. But I'm a tough fellow so don't count on outliving me, even if you can give me five years." This drew something between a snort and a chuckle. "Of course I won't be happy about it, but if it'll make you feel better to die first, I suppose I can make the sacrifice."

"Oh, Max!" There were tears in her eyes. "I love you very much."

"As long as that is so, I know we'll be happy. I know because I waited thirty years to meet a woman who could touch my heart. I took one look at you in the Petworth assembly room and knew I had found her. I'm a very steadfast man and I will always love you. Not only that, but I will take the greatest care of you. I'll treat you even better than I treat my horses."

Her capable fists pummeled his chest. "You are outrageous! Next you'll be threatening to ride me."

"I already have. And you can ride me too." He watched her construe his meaning and her mouth widened to a wicked grin that sent a message to his cock. "I think the waiting time is down to five minutes. You are about to learn, my darling, about some more of the advantages of marriage." He pulled her down into his arms and she snuggled into his side, her head in the crook of his neck.

"Max."

"Yes?"

"I'm sorry. That I never read your letters. We could have been married for years. I'm so glad we met again."

"Don't dwell on it anymore. Let's think about what's to come. It's very lucky you're such a managing woman. I have dozens of relations who need your assistance."

"I'm no longer so confident in my ability to improve the affairs of others."

"Nonsense. We'll be able to combine visits to our families with my calls on horse buyers. Though, if you don't mind, we won't stay with the Ashdowns when we're in Sussex."

"Poor Sylvia." She kissed his collarbone. "What about the children? Our children?"

"We'll take them with us."

"You're quite mad." He felt a wet drop on his shoulder.

"What's this? Tears? I shall have to do something about them."

"I'm not crying." She sniffed. "I'm happy."

Eleanor woke feeling better than she ever had in her life, despite aching muscles and a certain soreness down below. The bustle outside told her the inn was enjoying a busy morning. Enough light seeped through the curtains to reveal her sleeping husband. Not legally hers, yet, but in a little while they'd drive to the border and make it official. And find Caro.

Good lord, Caro! She'd completely forgotten.

"Wake up, Max." Even shaking his bare shoulder gave her a frisson of pleasure. Pity there wasn't time to do anything else this morning except dress and eat.

Without opening his eyes he pulled her to him for a kiss. Any interesting development was forestalled by a knock at the door. She ducked beneath the sheet. Thank God the servants thought they were already married.

"We'll just go in and surprise them," she heard.

Caro! *Caro?*

"Wait!" She slid to the floor and rummaged through her valise for the nightdress she'd never got around to wearing. "Put this on." She tossed Max his shirt.

He made no effort to leave the bed, but put on the garment in obedience to her furious glare. "The managing begins," he murmured.

She was scarcely decent when the door opened to admit Caro and Robert Townsend, looking radiant with youth and beauty and entirely unashamed of themselves.

"Eleanor!" Caro said.

"Max!" said Robert.

Eleanor wondered how, as the supposed responsible

adults, they were going to explain themselves. But Caro was no more interested in the affairs of her elders than she ever had been.

"Guess what! We were married last night. Isn't it a beautiful day?" She sat on the edge of the bed and started a rambling account of their journey, punctuated with excited exclamations about the wonders of Robert, who regarded her with amusement. Not knowing him well, Eleanor couldn't say if his affection equaled that of his bride. But Max was right. In her own current state of happiness she couldn't find it in herself to regard their future with misgivings.

"How did you find us?" she asked, when Caro had finished her rapturous account of their Scottish wedding.

"We drove from Gretna this morning and stopped to hire a post chaise when we learned Mr. and Mrs. Quinton were staying in the inn. When did you get married? Did you go to Gretna, too?"

Eleanor glanced at Max, a silently smiling observer of the scene. He shrugged.

"Well, we aren't married yet. But we will be later today."

"Darling Eleanor!" Caro cried, evincing no shock at the behavior of her erstwhile chaperone. "I wish you happy and so does Robert, don't you Robert?"

"Felicitations, madam. And to you Max."

"Would you come back with us to Scotland and witness *our* wedding?" Eleanor asked. "I wanted to be there for yours, but you got here much sooner than I expected."

"No," Max interrupted. "We're not going to Gretna Green. We shall return to Lancashire, have the banns called, and be respectably married by your father. Robert and Caro will come with us and with luck people will think they were married there too. The elopement can be hushed up."

Eleanor gazed at him fondly. "How clever of Max. I want you to be received in society, Caro."

Caro shook her head in disbelief, as though Eleanor were the foolish youngster. "I told you we don't care about the *ton*. We're going down to London to meet the others and see Robert's banker and attend a sale of pictures at Christie's." She took Robert's hand and smiled blissfully.

"That's right," Robert agreed. "Now that Max doesn't control the purse strings, I can buy any picture I want."

"And I can buy new clothes that weren't chosen by Mama."

"Then we thought we'd run over to Amsterdam. Caro's never been abroad."

"And then we're going to buy a house in London."

"Too bad we can't go to Paris."

"Oh Eleanor!" Caro said, leaning over to give her a hug. "I told you love was delicious."

"Good Lord, Max," Eleanor said, once the newly married couple had taken their leave with well-meaning promises to write that would surely be broken. "I don't know whether to laugh or cry."

Max, who had remained in bed throughout the entire visit, seized her hand and pulled her down beside him. She relaxed into his reliable solidity.

"If things don't go well, you will be there to set them right."

"We," she said. "We'll do it together."

"So laugh, because it's the only rational thing to do."

"Thank God I'm marrying a sensible man."

Want to know what happens when
fun-loving Caro grows up?
Keep reading for an excerpt from

THE IMPORTANCE OF BEING WICKED

available December 2012
from Miranda Neville
and
Avon Books

CHAPTER ONE

Spring 1800

They'd reached the rump of the evening. Caro Townsend surveyed the remains of another dinner party. No one had much to say, but no one wanted to brave the cold streets of London in the small hours. How small the hour was she had no idea; the mantel clock was unreliable at the best of times and had no chance of being right when she forgot to wind it. Half a dozen guests remained in the drawing room of Caro's Conduit Street house. In one corner, an argument between two painters and a writer on the superiority of their respective arts had degenerated into desultory insults. Adam and Lydia Longley, exhausted by their roles in a reenactment of Hogarth's *Rake's Progress*, had collapsed on the sofa like a pair of puppies. And Oliver Bream was drunk.

"May I tell you a secret, Caro?" he asked, sprawling on the floor at her feet.

"Of course." Caro tried not to laugh. She knew what was coming, and it was no secret to anyone.

"I'm in love," the young artist said earnestly.

She rolled her eyes and fortified herself with another gulp of wine in preparation for an oft-told tale.

"I'm in love with Lady Windermere," he said, then lowered his voice to a reverent whisper. "With Cynthia."

"I would never have guessed."

Oliver was too far gone to detect sarcasm. "She's the loveliest, sweetest woman in the entire world. She's perfect." He looked around the room, puckish disappointment creasing his face. "But she left."

"She owns a carriage, Oliver. When you order a carriage for a certain hour, you have to leave."

"That's dreadful. We're lucky not to keep carriages."

Caro had always found a coach most convenient. But since she preferred not to dwell on her reduced circumstances, she emptied her glass and continued to listen to Oliver's ramblings. She needed to send the rest of the party home or face the wrath of Mrs. Batten in the morning. Her few servants were immensely tolerant, but the housekeeper became tetchy about sleeping bodies when the maid had to clean the room. Caro never wished to speed the parting guest. She hated the moment when the last one left and she was alone again.

Oliver finally ran out of words to laud the charms of his latest inamorata. "Now you know my secret. It's your turn to tell me one."

"My life is an open book. I'm widowed, disreputable, and poor. What else is there to know?"

"Everyone has secrets."

There *was* something, one thing that she, and no one else, knew. She'd kept it to herself for over a year now, since the day she was widowed. She'd never even told Oliver, her best friend and supporter since Robert's death.

Caro looked about her; no one else paid any attention to them. She bent over Oliver's tousled head and whispered, "Promise you won't tell anyone."

"If I tell a single soul, may I be doomed forever to paint nothing but children and dogs." Coming from Oliver, who had very definite notions of the proper subject matter for a serious artist, this was a powerful oath.

She knew she shouldn't, but suddenly the knowledge was like a weight on her spirit. "I own a Titian."

Oliver shook his head sadly. "No, Caro. You're confused. Robert sold his Titian. Shame, because it was a great painting."

"He didn't. I just told everyone he had."

"Truly? Why isn't it hanging in its old place, then? May I see it? Where is it?"

Damn! Oliver was much too interested. She recalled now how much he'd always admired the naked Venus. "It's hidden. I shouldn't have told you. Remember! No word to anyone."

She stood abruptly, praying Oliver was too drunk to remember in the morning. "Friends," she commanded, clapping her hands smartly. "This evening has become a bore."

The company sprang to bleary attention, even the Longleys waking from their doze.

"As you know, my cousin arrives next week to stay with me. Annabella is a young lady of impeccable breeding and is being courted by a duke."

The artistic set affected Jacobin tendencies, so the statement evoked a chorus of "No duke, no dukes."

Caro raised her hand. "Since I am shortly to become a

chaperone and respectable"—jeers of disbelief—"I propose a little excursion. We'll climb over the railings into Hyde Park and bathe in the Serpentine."

Cries of horror echoed throughout the room. "You're mad, Caro!" "We'll die of cold."

"Very well. If you're all such old ladies, I shall sing to you instead."

"No!"

"Spare our ears."

"Death would be preferable."

So the evening ended, like so many before it, with an act of dubious legality and undeniable insanity. The cold-water bath stirred Caro's blood. Shivering in her cloak on the bank of the lake, she thought how lucky she was to have such wonderful friends.

A week later

Sir Bernard Horner appeared to be a disreputable man, not surprising since he claimed to have been a friend and gaming partner of Robert Townsend. Lack of respectability, infamy even, didn't necessarily bother Robert's widow. But Caro didn't like the look of Horner.

He was handsome enough, she supposed. His clothes fit *very* well, buff pantaloons hugging every contour of his legs in a manner unsuited to his advanced years. His short-waisted coat was made from a striped twill that was a shade too loud. The curls in his brown hair did not appear to be natural and contrasted oddly with the pale face of a man who spent long nights in gaming hells. Caro had never seen or heard of the fellow, but that was typical of the company Robert kept in the last year or two of his life, when his passion for the gaming tables tore him from home most of the time, neglecting his former intimates and his own wife.

"Why have you only come to me now, Sir Bernard?" she asked. "Why not make the claim immediately after my husband's death?"

"I didn't like to harass his grieving widow."

"How thoughtful of you to postpone your harassment until now."

Horner tried to look wounded, an unconvincing expression that merely made him appear reptilian. "Robert did owe me a thousand pounds."

Caro defied the sinking of her stomach. "You must think me naïve. Gaming debts are not legally enforceable."

"Quite right. That is why I declined to accept his vowels. He signed a loan."

Even without close examination, Caro could see that the document he held was horribly official-looking. She'd seen enough loan instruments to recognize the tax stamp at a glance. "You lent my husband a large sum of money, then proceeded to win it from him at hazard?"

"That was his choice. I didn't force him to cast the devil's bones with me." No one ever had to force Robert to lose money. He had a veritable genius for it.

She switched tactics. "Sir Bernard," she said in the wheedling tone she'd practiced on importunate tradesmen for years. "I'm afraid I do not have a thousand pounds to give you. I live now under very modest circumstances."

"Don't forget the interest. The total is now closer to eleven hundred." He bared his teeth, probably intending—and failing—to look sympathetic. She knew what was coming. The rumor had spread through the neighborhood like fire. She'd already had three merchants trying to collect the full amount owed them, based on garbled repetition of Oliver's indiscretion.

"I hear you own a very valuable picture," Horner said. "I would be prepared to take the *Farnese Venus* in full settlement of the debt."

"How many times must I tell people," she said, "that my husband sold the Venus before he died." She groped for her handkerchief and dabbed at her eyes. "If you heard I possessed such a painting, the report doubtless referred to that one." She pointed to the canvas hanging on the far wall of the drawing room, cast in shadow by the angle of the late-afternoon light. "It's the work of Mr. Oliver Bream, my tenant at the carriage house. Anyone with the most cursory knowledge of art will tell you it was painted recently, not two hundred years ago."

Her unwelcome visitor's lascivious gaze settled on the almost naked woman, reclining on a satin-draped divan most excellently rendered from the painter's imagination, Oliver not being in a position to afford such a costly prop.

"Posed for it yourself, did you?"

"Certainly not! How dare you suggest it?"

Horner's skepticism was patent. "It looks like you."

She wondered if that was how she appeared to others, looking straight at the viewer with a distinctly come-hither expression. But the goddess's lush curves and full rose-nippled breasts were most definitely not hers. And even if they were, Horner was in no position to judge. She trusted she'd never be desperate enough to give him the opportunity to see her unclothed.

"It's just the hair," she said. "My husband originally bought the Titian because she had red hair like mine."

"Why did he sell it then?"

Caro wiped her eyes again and gave a pitiful little sniff. "You need hardly ask. You are aware of his financial difficulties."

"Mighty fishy how the most valuable painting he owned disappeared just before his death."

"I don't know for certain, but I think he lost it, or sold it, to his good friend Marcus Lithgow."

"Who promptly left the country. Convenient that."

"Naturally, the loss of the painting that meant so much to me caused me great pain. I asked Mr. Bream to try and reproduce it, and he made the hair as short as mine is now."

"So it was done lately?"

Some of it very lately indeed. If her visitor's nose hovered closer to the canvas, he'd notice the tacky paint on the face and hair, hurriedly applied that morning.

"In the last year," Caro said. This morning was certainly in the last year.

"Strange that you can afford to buy a big picture like that yet can't find ten pounds to pay your coal bill."

"You seem remarkably well informed about my affairs, Sir Bernard."

"Just taking care of my interests, dear lady." He turned from the wall and fixed his eyes on Caro's bosom with a distinct gleam. This was an occasion on which she regretted her adoption of the scanty muslin fashions from France. "We may be able to come to a different arrangement, Mrs. Townsend. A fine woman like you must get lonely . . . at night."

Caro would have liked to slap the unctuous rascal. Or kick him somewhere painful. But she had to keep him on the right side of friendly, or he could cause her trouble. Caro owed a frightening amount of money to dozens of creditors, holders of the staggering bills run up by the Townsends during Robert's lifetime. Her late husband had been meticulous in paying his gambling debts but never paid a merchant if he could avoid it. When he died, it turned out the former had consumed most of his once-handsome fortune while the tradesmen's bills lingered on to bedevil his widow.

She once more had recourse to her handkerchief, dabbing delicately at the corner of one eye.

"I couldn't even consider such a notion, Sir Bernard, with poor, poor Robert dead little more than a year. But I am sure there are many ladies who would be flattered to have a fine gentleman like yourself pay your addresses."

She hoped her regard conveyed enough admiration to flatter the villain, combined with a shocked grief at his presumption. In fact, he looked disconcerted. Caro strongly suspected the existence of a Lady Horner and thus the impossibility of the horrid creature paying any addresses of an honest kind.

"Allow me to show you out."

He stayed her progress to the door with a hand on her shoulder. "The information I have is that there's a Titian in this house. Not just a painting of a naked woman."

For the first time since Horner had appeared at the front

door and talked his way past her manservant, Caro produced a genuine smile.

"Of course there is," she said, shaking off his touch. "Allow me to introduce him. Sir Bernard, meet Titian, known to his friends as Tish." She pointed at the striped ginger cat sprawled on the sofa.

"Your cat?" he said in disbelief?

Tish opened one golden eye and looked lazily at the visitor.

"My cat. And now you know that the rumors about the Titian are nonsense, I beg you will leave me in peace with my grief."

Though far from satisfied and not entirely convinced, there was nothing Horner could do but depart, not without an unnecessary kiss on her hand and a promise to call on her again soon.

Caro collapsed onto the sofa and sighed. Horner wasn't the first dun she'd had to repel that week, merely the most terrifying. The tradesmen she currently patronized for her household needs were more polite but no more inclined to issue her credit. Keeping herself and her small staff of servants fed, clothed, and warm was a constant struggle. She now had a houseguest too.

"What am I to do, Tish?" He rolled onto his back and started to purr as she rubbed his tummy. "What shall I sell next? It may have to be you, especially if you don't eat less."

Around the modest but well-proportioned salon hung Robert's principal legacy: the oil paintings, watercolors, and drawings he'd collected since he had been an Oxford undergraduate. Those of substantial value had been sold, but many remained: the works of young, unknown, or unpopular artists. Along with the house and her meager income, she'd been permitted to keep them, but only because none of them would make so much as a pinhole in the remaining mountain of debt.

Except the Titian. The only one she truly cared for.

Robert's former guardian had negotiated payment arrangements which she found hard to meet while continuing to live within her slender means. She still owed large sums and now this new and enormous obligation. If she didn't pacify Horner, he could summon the debt collectors again. Possibly more efficient ones than had previously searched the house.

She tore upstairs to her bedroom and found the secret catch. A section of painted paneling opened, the door to a closet visible only to one who knew about it.

Her irrationally pounding heart calmed. It was still there.

Caro stepped into the tiny octagonal room, cunningly fit into the junction of three second-floor rooms. Even the servants were ignorant of its existence. As soon as he'd seen the secret closet, Robert had wanted the house, though small for their needs and on an unfashionable street. The notion of a private cabinet, such as had been possessed by many royal collectors, tickled his fancy. He'd kept some of his more *outré* works of art there, and since his death, it had been home to the *Farnese Venus*, one of Titian's most appealing works.

She lay, all creamy flesh and sensuous curves, on a bed of crimson velvet, her son, the infant Cupid, playing at her feet. They'd bought it together, from a French émigré count, to celebrate their marriage. Even in the days of the 1790s, when fleeing French aristocrats let priceless treasures go for a song, the Titian had commanded a princely price. Robert said the goddess looked like her, with her red-gold locks and creamy skin tones. She didn't, of course. Caro was a diminutive redhead, pretty but no true beauty. Still, the Venus remained special to the Townsends, a souvenir of rapturous honeymoon days.

When she first saw it, the pose was what caught her attention. She would imitate the goddess for Robert, dressing her red hair in the same way and arranging her undressed figure for his delectation and seduction. The child god had been a charming irrelevancy. Now she avoided looking at him for a different reason. He was a bittersweet reminder that she'd lost her own son as well as his father.

She'd lied and cheated her creditors by holding on to the Titian, even when its sale would clear many of her debts. Caro couldn't let go of the tangible proof that she had once meant something to her husband, before he'd been consumed by his passion for the dice. Before his short life had come to an inglorious end of a fever caught gaming for forty-eight hours straight in a low hell in Seven Dials. It was foolish, perhaps, but with Robert gone and no child, she felt if she lost the Venus, her whole life would lose its meaning.

She bid the Venus a silent farewell. Hearing her name called, she looked over the banister and saw a mop of fair curls at the foot of the stairs.

"I saw him leave," Oliver said.

"I fobbed him off. For now."

"Well done! What did he think of my Venus?"

"Artists! Do you honestly care what a man like Horner thinks? All he cares about is money."

"He's the first man to see it. Was he overcome by her beauty?"

"He was struck by her resemblance to me. How could you, Oliver? First you blab all over town that I own a picture that was supposed to have been sold ages ago. Now he'll no doubt start a rumor that I posed naked for you." In fact, Oliver had taken an unfinished canvas, abandoned when he could no longer afford to pay the model, and adapted it.

His boyish feature wore nothing but wounded innocence. "The whole point was that the hair is like yours."

"You didn't have to make it short! When Robert said the Titian reminded him of me, my hair was long."

"I'm sorry. I never thought of that."

As they talked they'd returned to the drawing room and now stood before the nude. Caro shook her head in despair. "I do trust that isn't my expression. She looks as though she is ready to welcome all comers. Horner had quite the wrong idea."

"No, not you. I was inspired by someone else."

"Oliver! Surely you don't mean Anne! I swear, she's never worn an expression like that in her life."

Oliver wore the fatuous grin provoked by Caro's cousin and current houseguest, Anne Brotherton, the latest unattainable object of his desire. "In my dreams, she does. One day, I know, she'll look at me like that."

Poor Oliver. He suffered hopeless passions, never with the slightest hint of reciprocation from their objects. His adoration of Cynthia, Lady Windermere, had lasted only a few days, but there was no point saying he'd be over Anne within the month. While in the throes of his fickle infatuations, he was convinced his love would last forever and eventually melt the lady-du-jour's obdurate heart. Caro reminded herself that she was not feeling sympathetic toward Oliver's absurdities today.

"I'm still very angry at you." Her voice broke with frustration. "How could you be so indiscreet, Oliver? I told you the Titian was a secret."

"I'm sorry I told Johnson. I've told him it was all nonsense. He won't say anything else, I promise. You know what happens when I get foxed."

Caro always found it hard to stay annoyed at Oliver. "I was at fault too. I drank too much wine that night."

"I'm glad you still have her. She's such an amazing work. How did Titian manage those skin tones?" He rocked back on his heels and squinted at his own work. "Mind you, I think *my* Venus is a damned good painting."

"It is," Caro assured him. "The flesh is beautifully painted."

"She is my masterpiece. I'm glad she'll be displayed in your drawing room. Someone may see her and want to buy her."

The painting was supposed to make up for the fact that Oliver owed her quite a large sum of money, amassed through small loans, a few pounds here and there to buy paints, canvas, or food. At present, he actually lived in the room over the carriage house as well as working there, having been ejected from his lodgings for nonpayment of rent. He didn't pay her rent, either. It was some time since he'd sold a picture. Caro was too softhearted to remind him that his Venus belonged, by rights, to her. Lord knows she'd never sell it, so if he found a buyer he might as well reap the reward.

Now that she knew of his inspiration, Caro could see some resemblance to Anne, despite her cousin's dark hair.

"I'm sure Annabella won't notice, but I wonder if Cynthia will see the likeness when she dines with me this evening."

"Let me dine with you too," he begged.

"You told me you were meeting Bartie St. James and the Longleys."

"We could all dine with you. Please? It'll be fun! Besides, none of us can afford to eat anywhere decent. Neither Bartie nor Adam Longley has sold a picture in weeks."

And I can't afford to feed every starving artist in London.

But she didn't say it. She never did. She loved her friends, and the Battens would come up with something. Robert's former valet and his wife, who combined the work of housekeeper and cook, had stayed with her despite the sometimes chaotic and often impecunious nature of her household. However short of money she might be, it was nothing to the poverty of Oliver and his friends. Besides, she and Robert had always kept an open house, and to do otherwise insulted his memory.

A house full keeps loneliness at bay.

"I'll speak to Mrs. Batten." She glanced at the clock and hoped it was right. "Good Lord! I must shoo you out of here! Annabella's duke will be here any moment."

"You're not going to let him marry her, are you?"

"Not unless he'll make her happy. Now go! I need to play the chaperone and terrify him."

Oliver grinned happily. "I don't want to miss that. I'll be back. I want to help."

Chapter Two

The Dukes of Castleton always married money. Since the first duke, a child of two, had been granted the title by his father Charles II, the family had been responsible for its own prosperity. The Merry Monarch was generous with titles and honors for his numerous mistresses and ever-growing crop of bastards, but he was also short of money. So the first Thomas Fitzcharles, son of an actress named Mary Swinburne, had a duke's title but an income scarcely worthy of the average baronet. He found himself a rich wife with a handsome estate and house in Hampshire, which he rechristened Castleton House.

His successors added to their holdings through judicious marriages until, a hundred years later, the family had amassed estates worthy of an earl and, better still, the income of a prosperous London merchant, but without the unfortunate necessity of anyone having to work for it. Not for the Dukes of Castleton the distasteful tasks of service to the Crown in the army or government. Instead, their talents were directed to the onerous business of seeking, pursuing, and winning the very best heiresses.

The fourth duke had always felt it keenly that his bride brought good blood but a mere twelve thousand pounds. In a moment of weakness, he'd been distracted by a pretty face. The marriage had not been a success. His son, he swore, would do better. It was with the greatest satisfaction that, on his deathbed, he heard of the demise of the only male heir to the enormously rich Earl of Camber, leaving the earl's granddaughter with a huge inheritance and no fiancé. "She's the one," he said happily, and expired.

His son, another Thomas Fitzcharles and the fifth duke, was on his way to meet his destiny: the Honorable Anne Brotherton. The fact that she was to be found in this plain gray brick house on a quiet street in Mayfair was surprising. But he supposed that Mrs. Townsend, Miss Brotherton's cousin, was a widowed lady of advanced years and retired habits. He'd never encountered her during his occasional incursions into the *ton*. She probably owned cats and rarely went out in society. Good. It was a trifle tiresome that Miss Brotherton insisted on coming to London at this time instead of letting him visit and woo her at her country estate. Thomas wasn't fond of London. And in the country there'd be no competition for the heiress's hand.

He paused on the steps and frowned, reluctant to request admittance despite a chilly drizzle. He wished he could summon more enthusiasm for the task at hand. But he'd always been a dutiful son and a dutiful Fitzcharles. And if he had it in mind to shirk either duty, his father's legacy had deprived him of the possibility of defiance. There was an irony in there somewhere should he wish to disinter it. But the Fitzcharleses didn't go in for irony, or any other fancy attitudes. Thomas was first and last a Fitzcharles, the Duke of Castleton, and his prime duty was to find a duchess. A rich duchess. The richest of all. He was sure he and Miss Brotherton would understand each other and deal very well. A spark of a notion that life and matrimony might hold something more was ignored. When he had time, he'd make sure it was snuffed out completely.

He grasped the brass door knocker and rapped it sharply. The manservant expected him and led him upstairs to a drawing room. He had an immediate impression of bright colors and a warm atmosphere that came from something more than the fire in the grate. The room held but a single occupant, a young woman. Was Miss Brotherton receiving him alone? It seemed most improper, though a hopeful sign for his courtship.

She set aside an embroidery frame, rose from the sofa, and moved forward to greet him, her hand outstretched.

"Your Grace," she said. He'd been a duke for over a year, but it was as though he'd never heard those two familiar words before. Her voice was a melody played on a clarinet, a fine brandy on a cold night.

As she dropped into a curtsey, he took her slender white hand and, instead of merely bowing, he raised it to his mouth, unthinkingly brushing his lips over her soft skin. An indefinable scent tickled his senses, and he wanted to pursue it. He didn't want to let her go.

She retrieved her hand and stepped back, leaving him a touch bereft. His spirits soared as he examined his intended bride. He saw a small woman—not much below average height, but he was a large man—clad in a soft white gown that displayed the pleasing proportions of her figure. Her only adornment was a thin red ribbon about her neck, but the simplicity of her dress enhanced her prettiness. Golden red curls framed a delicate face with a faint dusting of freckles over a sweet little nose. Both her eyes, somewhere between gold and brown, and her dark rose mouth sent the message of humor and enjoyment of life. The smile that animated her expression roused a warm tightness in his chest and a certain heat farther down his body. He felt his lips stretch into a foolish answering grin. Then she spoke again.

"Anne is at the dressmaker's. I am her cousin, Caro Townsend."

The room suddenly felt as chilly as the street outside. Fool that he was. Miss Brotherton was no redhead. Every report said she was a pretty dark-haired girl. Which, describing an heiress, meant she was no more than passable and probably plain. Had this glorious creature—the widowed cousin—been an heiress, she'd have been lauded as a raving beauty in every corner of the kingdom.

Disappointment, scarcely acknowledged, turned to annoyance that his quarry hadn't the courtesy to receive him. "Honored, ma'am," he said, his words as stiff as his spine. "You should have sent word that the time of my call did not suit."

"Oh it suited," she said blithely. "Anne will return soon. I wanted to meet you first."

"I have the permission of her guardian to call on Miss Brotherton. Doubtless Lord Morrissey wrote to you himself."

Her laugh was as smoky as her voice. "Morrissey has no idea Anne is with me. He doesn't approve of me."

"I'm sure you exaggerate, ma'am."

"Unfortunately not. I'm held in quite low repute. You must not have asked anyone about me."

"I confess I understood you to be a lady of more ... advanced years since you were cousin to Miss Brotherton's late father."

"My father married late, my cousin early, so the generations slipped out of alignment. I'm four years older than dear Annabella, though she used to call me aunt as a joke."

"You don't look anything like my aunts."

"I'll take that as a compliment. I think. Let's sit down, Duke. My cousin is very dear to me, and I am her chaperone. Imagine I'm that frightening old lady you'd been expecting and let me ask you some difficult questions."

He wasn't sure whether to be amused or indignant. This little slip of a girl appeared quite serious about interrogating a duke.

"May I offer you refreshment? A glass of wine?"

"Thank you, no. I need to keep my wits about me."

He waited for her to be seated, then, following her gesture, lowered himself onto a sofa, almost sitting on a massive ginger cat who lay there on his back, his four legs splayed to display a white stomach.

"Don't mind Tish," she said.

He squeezed himself into the corner of the sofa so as not to disturb the sleeping beast. At last, some aspect of his imagined picture of the Widow Townsend turned out to be accurate.

"Handsome creature. Tish, did you say?"

"Short for Atishoo. He sneezes a lot." The cat opened his eyes and stared at Thomas without moving from its undignified position. "Do you like cats?"

"I prefer dogs," he said tactfully, rather hoping the creature wasn't about to live up to its name all over his breeches.

The room had a cheerful atmosphere. The clutter of feminine occupation lay everywhere: sewing, books, a sketchbook. A vase of red tulips echoed the shades of an oriental carpet. Despite the unwelcome feline company, his seat was a comfortable one. He relaxed and waited confidently for Mrs. Townsend to do her worst.

Mrs. Townsend leaned forward in her chair. "How old are you?" she asked.

"That's a delicate question."

"Of a woman, yes. A gentleman has nothing to hide about his years except perhaps a lack of them. Besides, the information is readily available in the peerage. Save me a visit to the circulating library."

"I am twenty-nine."

"I see."

Mrs. Townsend stood up and moved to take a seat at a writing desk, sideways to the room so she presented her profile. Having dipped her pen in the inkpot, she wrote something down, something that took longer than inscribing two digits. He watched her, taking in a cluster of curls at her forehead, a small, slightly upturned nose, and a mischievous mouth. It occurred to him she was toying with him.

"Is that good or bad?" he asked finally, breaking the silence against his better judgment.

She turned her head. "It remains to be seen. Tell me of your family. Where do they—and you—live?"

"I have three sisters, the eldest of whom is married. The two youngest, twins of sixteen years, live with me at my principal residence, Castleton Park, near Basingstoke in Hampshire. As does my mother," he added. "The estate there has some five thousand acres." He wondered if she expected him to tell her his income, something he'd rather avoid for the present. "I own town properties in Guildford as well as lands in Wiltshire, Surrey, Hertfordshire, Suffolk, and Lincolnshire."

"Three addresses inspire confidence, six is a little excessive. Do you own a London house, too?"

"Fitzcharles House is in Whitehall. It is currently let, but I expect to repossess it once I am wed. In town I stay at Nerot's Hotel."

"So you don't spend much time in London?"

"I haven't until now. While my father lived, I spent much of my time traveling to our different estates when I wasn't at home. Although I prefer the country, I expect to attend Parliament now that I am duke."

"I hope you wouldn't expect a wife to bury herself in rural obscurity."

"I am willing to accommodate Miss Brotherton's desires, but surely she has spent much of her life in the country."

"Very true, unfortunately. Anne has come to visit me to get a taste of town life."

She began to write again, or at least scratch at the paper. He couldn't imagine what she was recording.

"I understood," he said, "that your cousin was not making a formal presentation."

"True. I shall not be presenting her at court at this time."

"So she won't be participating much in the entertainments of the season?"

Mrs. Townsend's pen continued to move. "I wouldn't say that. I daresay we shall manage to amuse ourselves."

"In that case," he said, "I would be honored to accompany you both to the assembly at Almack's next Wednesday."

"I'm sure that would be most entertaining." Setting down her pen with a click, she shifted her chair to face him. "What do you do, Duke? How do you spend your time?"

"I tend to the duties of my situation in life."

"I'm sure you are a paragon among dukes." She sounded impatient. "What gives you pleasure? What gladdens your heart?"

What kind of questions were these? Was this a trap? "Well," he said, pondering how he should respond, "I take pride in my stables and maintain a small racing establishment at Newmarket. Nothing extravagant," he added quickly, lest she think him given to profligacy. "I rarely wager. I play cards only for small stakes, and I drink wine in moderation."

"That all sounds very dull. Do you keep a mistress?"

Good God in heaven! What kind of chaperone, of whatever age, asked a question like that? She seemed quite unaware of anything unusual, merely regarded him with raised eyebrows and a bold gaze. He couldn't meet it and looked away, casting desperately around the room for inspiration in answering, or not answering. What he found didn't help, but it did explain what kind of woman *asked* such a thing.

A woman whose portrait—whose *stark-naked* portrait—hung on the wall of her drawing room where anyone might see it. He tried to look away, but he couldn't. Not so much as a wisp of fabric veiled the expanse of pale flesh. He wrenched his attention away from the depiction of his hostess's exposed body to the painted face, which wore an expression not so dissimilar to that the original had recently fixed on him. Bold indeed. Except that as he gazed at the picture, the look in the woman's eyes seemed to grow sensual, inviting, unlike his hostess's quizzical expression. He twisted his neck, which felt warm under its encasing layers of linen.

He darted a look back at Mrs. Townsend and stopped. It was not, it occurred to him, a very good likeness, aside from the coiffure, the shockingly short red curls.

Perhaps he was wrong about the model. Trying not to be obvious about it, he compared the unclothed reclining body with the muslin-clad figure seated at the escritoire. Surely the painting's figure was more voluptuous. Were her breasts not quite a bit larger? Mrs. Townsend, he realized, knew what was going through his head, and she was laughing at him. He felt himself flush with embarrassment at being caught staring at her bosom.

"Is it you?" he mumbled.

"What do you think?"

"I don't know. If it is, the painter is no great hand at a likeness. You aren't that plump." He cringed as the words emerged, but she didn't seem offended. She was a most unusual woman.

In fact, she was quite unlike anyone he'd ever met in his life. For all the grandeur of his birth and rank, Thomas was, he knew, a simple man, almost a country bumpkin, except that no one would ever insult a duke so. Mrs. Townsend was the opposite, a lady used to the artificial style of town life. The ingenuous curls and plain white gown he'd initially seen as the simple attire suitable to a young girl were in fact quite the opposite, evidence of polished sophistication such as he'd never encountered. He couldn't envision any of his sisters dressed like that. Or speaking thus. He should think not!

He stared at her, perplexed by how to deal with her.

Caro stared back at the duke, holding back open mirth with some difficulty. Her interrogation had been intended to embarrass him and had succeeded. His reaction to the picture was a bonus.

None of her friends would find the picture shocking, whether or not it depicted her. She'd forgotten the prudery of so much of the world. And this man, she had no doubt, possessed more than his fair share of that dismal virtue. A pity. Her initial impression of him had been unwillingly positive. She'd even detected a hint of dry humor. *You don't look anything like my aunts.* She'd swear his lips had twitched when he said it. But his recitation of his assets and qualities had reignited her fear that poor Annabella might find herself wed to a damnably dull dog.

She shouldn't have mentioned his mistress. It was the kind of thing that upset stuffy types. He probably didn't have one, the dried-up prune. She'd surely teased him enough, but for some reason she very much wanted to know.

"You didn't answer my question," she said. "Do you keep a mistress?"

"You haven't answered *my* question," he retorted. "Is that you?" He pointed at the picture.

"I don't think it's any of your business."

"Precisely."

She leaped to her feet. Even irritated, his manners were so instinctive he didn't remain seated when she stood. He towered over her, and she noted again that he was a big man. Tall and solid, with broad shoulders and chest tapering to narrow hips and well-muscled legs. His clothing, like the cut of his brown hair, was distinguished only by tasteful propriety. His features were pleasant without being excessively handsome, his eyes an ordinary blue. Though she had noticed unusually long and thick dark eyelashes. Looking for the key to his character in his appearance, she found nothing but dignified reserve exemplified by the stillness of his hands. Unlike hers, with her constant fidgeting, her need to keep busy with embroidery. So she'd pressed him with her questions, trying to provoke a reaction.

She'd succeeded but couldn't flatter herself she'd learned much except that his attitudes were as provincial as his tailoring. She glared at him and he glared back, his breathing a little elevated. The atmosphere in the room seemed thick with some unnamed emotion. Probably disgust.

When he spoke his tone was measured. "I find your inquiry impertinent, Mrs. Townsend. But I'll grant you the benefit of the doubt and assume it is motivated by concern for your cousin's future happiness rather than prurient interest. I will tell you this much. Once married, I will be true to my wife. She will have no cause for concern."

While she couldn't object to such a sentiment, it wasn't her plan to show him any approval. He needed to do much more to convince her he was the right man for Anne. But his cutting response left her momentarily at a loss for words. Luckily, a door closing and a commotion downstairs informed her that Anne had returned.

About the Author

MIRANDA NEVILLE grew up in England before moving to New York City to work in Sotheby's rare books department. After many years as a journalist and editor she decided writing fiction was more fun. She lives in Vermont. For more about Miranda please visit her website www.mirandaneville.com.

Visit www.AuthorTracker.com for exclusive information on your favorite HarperCollins authors.

Give in to your impulses . . .
Read on for a sneak peek at two brand-new
e-book original tales of romance
from Avon Books.
Available now wherever e-books are sold.

THE FORBIDDEN LADY
By Kerrelyn Sparks

TURN TO DARKNESS
By Jaime Rush

An Excerpt from

THE FORBIDDEN LADY

by Kerrelyn Sparks

(Originally published under
the title *For Love or Country*)

Before *New York Times* bestselling author Kerrelyn Sparks
created a world of vampires, there was another world of spies
and romance . . .

Keep reading for a look at her very first novel.

CHAPTER ONE

Tuesday, August 29, 1769

"I say, dear gel, how much do *you* cost?"

Virginia's mouth dropped open. "I—I beg your pardon?"

The bewigged, bejeweled, and bedeviling man who faced her spoke again. "You're a fetching sight and quite sweet-smelling for a wench who has traveled for weeks, imprisoned on this godforsaken ship. I say, what *is* your price?"

She opened her mouth, but nothing came out. The rolling motion of the ship caught her off guard, and she stumbled, widening her stance to keep her balance. This man thought she was for sale? Even though they were on board *The North Star,* a brigantine newly arrived in Boston Harbor with a fresh supply of indentured servants, could he actually mistake her for one of the poor wretched criminals huddled near the front of the ship?

Her first reaction of shock was quickly replaced with anger. It swelled in her chest, heated to a quick boil, and soared past her ruffled neckline to her face, scorching her cheeks 'til she fully expected steam, instead of words, to escape her mouth.

"How . . . how *dare* you!" With gloved hands, she twisted the silken cords of her drawstring purse. "Pray, be gone with you, sir."

"Ah, a saucy one." The gentleman plucked a silver snuff-box from his lavender silk coat. He kept his tall frame erect to avoid flipping his wig, which was powdered with a lavender tint to match his coat. "Tsk, tsk, dear gel, such impertinence is sure to lower your price."

Her mouth fell open again.

Seizing the opportunity, he raised his quizzing glass and examined the conveniently opened orifice. "Hmm, but you do have excellent teeth."

She huffed. "And a sharp tongue to match."

"*Mon Dieu*, a very saucy mouth, indeed." He smiled, displaying straight, white teeth.

A perfectly bright smile, Virginia thought. What a pity his mental faculties were so dim in comparison. But she refrained from responding with an insulting remark. No good could come from stooping to his level of ill manners. She stepped back, intending to leave, but hesitated when he spoke again.

"I do so like your nose. Very becoming and—" He opened his silver box, removed a pinch of snuff with his gloved fingers and sniffed.

She waited for him to finish the sentence. He was a buffoon, to be sure, but she couldn't help but wonder—did he actually like her nose? Over the years, she had endured a great deal of teasing because of the way it turned up on the end.

He snapped his snuffbox shut with a click. "Ah, yes, where was I, becoming and . . . disdainfully haughty. Yes, that's it."

Heat pulsed to her face once more. "I daresay it is not surprising for *you* to admire something *disdainfully haughty*, but regardless of your opinion, it is improper for you to address me so rudely. For that matter, it is highly improper for you to speak to me at all, for need I remind you, sir, we have not been introduced."

He dropped his snuffbox back into his pocket. "Definitely disdainful. And haughty." His mouth curled up, revealing two dimples beneath the rouge on his cheeks.

She glared at the offensive fop. Somehow, she would give him the cut he deserved.

A short man in a brown buckram coat and breeches scurried toward them. "Mr. Stanton! The criminals for sale are over there, sir, near the forecastle. You see the ones in chains?"

Raising his quizzing glass, the lavender dandy pivoted on his high heels and perused the line of shackled prisoners. He shrugged his silk-clad shoulders and glanced back at Virginia with a look of feigned horror. "Oh, dear, what a delightful little *faux pas*. I suppose you're not for sale after all?"

"No, of course not."

"I do beg your pardon." He flipped a lacy, monogrammed handkerchief out of his chest pocket and made a poor attempt to conceal the wide grin on his face.

A heavy, flowery scent emanated from his handkerchief, nearly bowling her over. He was probably one of those people who never bathed, just poured on more perfume. She covered her mouth with a gloved hand and gently coughed.

"Well, no harm done." He waved his handkerchief in the

air. "*C'est la vie* and all that. Would you care for some snuff? 'Tis my own special blend from London, don't you know. We call it *Grey Mouton*."

"Gray sheep?"

"Why, yes. Sink me! You *parlez français*? How utterly charming for one of your class."

Narrowing her eyes, she considered strangling him with the drawstrings of her purse.

He removed the silver engraved box from his pocket and flicked it open. "A pinch, in the interest of peace?" His mouth twitched with amusement.

"No, thank you."

He lifted a pinch to his nose and sniffed. "What did I tell you, Johnson?" he asked the short man in brown buckram at his side. "These Colonials are a stubborn lot, far too eager to take offense"—he sneezed delicately into his lacy handkerchief—"and far too unappreciative of the efforts the mother country makes on their behalf." He slid his closed snuffbox back into his pocket.

Virginia planted her hands on her hips. "You speak, perhaps, of Britain's kindness in providing us with a steady stream of slaves?"

"Slaves?"

She gestured toward the raised platform of the forecastle, where Britain's latest human offering stood in front, chained at the ankles and waiting to be sold.

"Oh." He waved his scented handkerchief in dismissal. "You mean the indentured servants. They're not slaves, my dear, only criminals paying their dues to society. 'Tis the mother country's fervent hope they will be reformed by their experience in America."

"I see. Perhaps we should send the mother country a boat-load of American wolves to see if they can be reformed by their experience in Britain?"

His chuckle was surprisingly deep. "*Touché.*"

The deep timbre of his voice reverberated through her skin, striking a chord that hummed from her chest down to her belly. She caught her breath and looked at him more closely. When his eyes met hers, his smile faded away. Time seemed to hold still for a moment as he held her gaze, quietly studying her.

The man in brown cleared his throat.

Virginia blinked and looked away. She breathed deeply to calm her racing heart. Once more, she became aware of the murmur of voices and the screech of sea gulls overhead. What had happened? It must have been the thrill of putting the man in his place that had affected her. Strange, though, that he had happily acknowledged her small victory.

Mr. Stanton gave the man in brown a mildly irritated look, then smiled at her once more. "American wolves, you say? Really, my dear, these people's crimes are too petty to compare them to murderous beasts. Why, Johnson, here, was an indentured servant before becoming my secretary. Were you not, Johnson?"

"Aye, Mr. Stanton," the older man answered. "But I came voluntarily. Not all these people are prisoners. The group to the right doesn't wear chains. They're selling themselves out of desperation."

"There, you see." The dandy spread his gloved hands, palms up, in a gesture of conciliation. "No hard feelings. In fact, I quite trust Johnson here with all my affairs in spite of his criminal background. You know the Colonials are quite wrong in thinking we British are a cold, callous lot."

Virginia gave Mr. Johnson a small, sympathetic smile, letting him know she understood his indenture had not been due to a criminal past. Her own father, faced with starvation and British cruelty, had left his beloved Scottish Highlands as an indentured servant. Her sympathy seemed unnecessary, however, for Mr. Johnson appeared unperturbed by his employer's rudeness. No doubt the poor man had grown accustomed to it.

She gave Mr. Stanton her stoniest of looks. "Thank you for enlightening me."

"My pleasure, dear gel. Now I must take my leave." Without further ado, he ambled toward the group of gaunt, shackled humans, his high-heeled shoes clunking on the ship's wooden deck and his short secretary tagging along behind.

Virginia scowled at his back. The British needed to go home, and the sooner, the better.

"I say, old man." She heard his voice filter back as he addressed his servant. "I do wish the pretty wench were for sale. A bit too saucy, perhaps, but I do so like a challenge. *Quel dommage*, a real pity, don't you know."

A vision of herself tackling the dandy and stuffing his lavender-tinted wig down his throat brought a smile to her lips. She could do it. Sometimes she pinned down her brother when he tormented her. Of course, such behavior might be frowned upon in Boston. This was not the hilly region of North Carolina that the Munro family called home.

And the dandy might prove difficult to knock down. Watching him from the back, she realized how large he was. She grimaced at the lavender bows on his high-heeled pumps. Why would a man that tall need to wear heels? Another pair of lavender bows served as garters, tied over the tabs of his silk knee breeches. His silken hose were too sheer to hide padding, so those calves were truly that muscular. *How odd.*

He didn't mince his steps like one would expect from a fopdoodle, but covered the deck with long, powerful strides, the walk of a man confident in his strength and masculinity.

She found herself examining every inch of him, calculating the amount of hard muscle hidden beneath the silken exterior. What color was his hair under that hideous tinted wig? Probably black, like his eyebrows. His eyes had gleamed like polished pewter, pale against his tanned face.

Her breath caught in her throat. A tanned face? A fop would not spend the necessary hours toiling in the sun that resulted in a bronzed complexion.

This Mr. Stanton was a puzzle.

She shook her head, determined to forget the perplexing man. Yet, if he dressed more like the men back home—tight buckskin breeches, boots, no wig, no lace . . .

The sun bore down with increasing heat, and she pulled her hand-painted fan from her purse and flicked it open. She breathed deeply as she fanned herself. Her face tingled with a mist of salty air and the lingering scent of Mr. Stanton's handkerchief.

She watched with growing suspicion as the man in question postured in front of the women prisoners with his quizzing glass, assessing them with a practiced eye. Oh, dear, what were the horrible man's intentions? She slipped her fan back into her purse and hastened to her father's side.

Jamie Munro was speaking quietly to a fettered youth who appeared a good five years younger than her one and twenty years. "All I ask, young man, is honesty and a good day's work. In exchange, ye'll have food, clean clothes, and a clean pallet."

The spindly boy's eyes lit up, and he licked his dry, chapped lips. "Food?"

Virginia's father nodded. "Aye. Mind you, ye willna be working for me, lad, but for my widowed sister, here, in Boston. Do ye have any experience as a servant?"

The boy lowered his head and shook it. He shuffled his feet, the scrape of his chains on the deck grating at Virginia's heart.

"Papa," she whispered.

Jamie held up a hand. "Doona fash yerself, lass. I'll be taking the boy."

As the boy looked up, his wide grin cracked the dried dirt on his cheeks. "Thank you, my lord."

Jamie winced. "Mr. Munro, it is. We'll have none of that lordy talk aboot here. Welcome to America." He extended a hand, which the boy timidly accepted. "What is yer name, lad?"

"George Peeper, sir."

"Father." Virginia tugged at the sleeve of his blue serge coat. "Can we afford any more?"

Jamie Munro's eyes widened and he blinked at his daughter. "More? Just an hour ago, ye upbraided me aboot the evils of purchasing people, and now ye want more? 'Tis no' like buying ribbons for yer bonny red hair."

"I know, but this is important." She leaned toward him. "Do you see the tall man in lavender silk?"

Jamie's nose wrinkled. "Aye. Who could miss him?"

"Well, he wanted to purchase me—"

"*What?*"

She pressed the palms of her hands against her father's broad chest as he moved to confront the dandy. "'Twas a misunderstanding. Please."

His blue eyes glittering with anger, Jamie clenched his fists. "Let me punch him for you, lass."

"No, listen to me. I fear he means to buy one of those ladies for . . . immoral purposes."

Jamie frowned at her. "And what would ye be knowing of a man's immoral purposes?"

"Father, I grew up on a farm. I can make certain deductions, and I know from the way he looked at me, the man is not looking for someone to scrub his pots."

"What can I do aboot it?"

"If he decides he wants one, you could outbid him."

"He would just buy another, Ginny. I canna be buying the whole ship. I can scarcely afford this one here."

She bit her lip, considering. "You could buy one more if Aunt Mary pays for George. She can afford it much more than we."

"Nay." Jamie shook his head. "I willna have my sister paying. This is the least I can do to help Mary before we leave.

Besides, I seriously doubt I could outbid the dandy even once. Look at the rich way he's dressed, though I havena stet clue why a man would spend good coin to look like that."

The ship rocked suddenly, and Virginia held fast to her father's arm. A breeze wafted past her, carrying the scent of unwashed bodies. She wrinkled her nose. She should have displayed the foresight to bring a scented handkerchief, though not as overpowering as the one sported by the lavender popinjay.

Having completed his leisurely perusal of the women, Mr. Stanton was now conversing quietly with a young boy.

"Look, Father, that boy is so young to be all alone. He cannot be more than ten."

"Aye," Jamie replied. "We can only hope a good family will be taking him in."

"How much for the boy?" Mr. Stanton demanded in a loud voice.

The captain answered, "You'll be thinking twice before taking that one. He's an expensive little wretch."

Mr. Stanton lowered his voice. "Why is that?"

"I'll be needing payment for his passage *and* his mother's. The silly tart died on the voyage, so the boy owes you fourteen years of labor."

The boy swung around and shook a fist at the captain. "Me mum was not a tart, ye bloody old bugger!"

The captain yelled back, "And he has a foul mouth, as you can see. You'll be taking the strap to him before the day is out."

Virginia squeezed her father's arm. "The boy is responsible for his mother's debt?"

"Aye." Jamie nodded. "'Tis how it works."

Mr. Stanton adjusted the lace on his sleeves. "I have a fancy to be extravagant today. Name your price."

"At least the poor boy will have a roof over his head and food to eat." Virginia grimaced. "I only hope the dandy will not dress him in lavender silk."

Jamie Munro frowned. "Oh, dear."

"What is it, Father?"

"Ye say the man was interested in you, Ginny?"

"Aye, he seemed to like me in his own horrid way."

"Hmm. Perhaps the lad will be all right. At any rate, 'tis too late now. Let me pay for George, and we'll be on our way."

An Excerpt from

TURN TO DARKNESS
by Jaime Rush

Enter the world of the Offspring with this latest novella in Jaime Rush's fabulous paranormal series.

CHAPTER ONE

When Shea Baker pulled into her driveway, the sight of Darius's black coupe in front of her little rented house annoyed her. That it wasn't Greer's Jeep, and that she was disappointed it wasn't, annoyed the hell out of her.

Darius pulled out his partially dismantled wheelchair from inside the car and put it together within a few seconds. His slide from the driver's seat into his wheelchair was so practiced it was almost fluid. He waved, oblivious to her frown, and wheeled over to her truck. "As pale as you looked after hearing what Tucker, Del, and I went through, I thought you'd go right home." He wore his dark blond hair in a James Dean style, his waves gelled to stand up.

She *had* been freaked. Two men trying to kill them, men who would kill them all if they knew about their existence. She yanked her baseball cap lower on her head, a nervous habit. "I had a couple of jobs to check on. What brings you by?" She hoped it was something quick he could tell her right there and leave.

"Tucker kicked me out. I think he feels threatened by me,

because I had to take charge. I saved the day, and he won't even admit it."

None of the guys were comfortable with Darius. His mercurial mood shifts and oversized ego were irritating, but the shadows in his eyes hinted at an affinity for violence. In the two years he'd lived with them, though, he'd mostly kept to himself. She'd had no problem with him because he remained aloof, never revealing his emotions, even when he talked about the car accident that had taken his mobility. Unfortunately, when he thought she was reaching out to him, that aloofness had changed to romantic interest.

"Sounded like you went off the rails." She crossed her arms in front of her. "Look, if you're here to get me on your side, I won't—"

"I'd never ask you to do that." His upper lip lifted in a sneer. "I know you're loyal only to Tucker."

She narrowed her eyes, her body stiffening. "Tuck's like a big brother to me. He gave me a home when I was on the streets, told me why I have extraordinary powers." That she'd inherited DNA from another dimension was crazy-wild, but it made as much sense as, say, being able to move objects with her mind. "I'd take his side over anyone's."

"Wish someone would feel that kind of loyalty to me," Darius muttered under his breath, making her wonder if he was trying to elicit her sympathy. "I get that you're brotherly/sisterly." He let those words settle for a second. "But something happened with you and Greer, didn't it? What did he do, grope you?"

"Don't be ridiculous. Greer would never do something like that."

"Something happened, because all of a sudden the way you looked at each other changed. Like he was way interested in you, and you were way uncomfortable around him. Then you sat all close to me, and I know you felt the same electricity I did."

She shook her head, sending her curly ponytail swinging over her shoulder. "There was no electricity. Greer and I had a . . . disagreement. I needed to put some space between us, but when you live in a house with four other people, there isn't a lot of room. When I sat next to you, I was just moving away from him."

Darius's shoulders, wide and muscular, stiffened. "You might think that, Shea. You might even believe it. But someday you're going to realize you want me. And when you do, I want you to know I can satisfy you. When I'm in Darkness, I'm a whole man." That dark glint in his eyes hinted at his arrogance. "I'm capable of anything."

Those words shivered through her, but not in the way he'd intended. In that moment, she knew somehow that he *was* capable of anything. Darius might be confined to a wheelchair, but only a fool would underestimate him, and she was no fool. Especially where Darkness was concerned. The guys possessed it, yet didn't know exactly what it was. All they knew was that they'd probably inherited it, along with the DNA that gave them extraordinary powers, from the men who'd gotten their mothers pregnant. It allowed them to Become something far from human.

"Please, Darius, don't talk to me about that kind of thing. I'm not interested in having sex with anyone."

The corner of his mouth twisted cruelly. "Don't you like

sex? Maybe you've never been with someone who could do it well."

For a long time the thought of sex had coated her in shame and disgust. Until that little incident with Greer, when she'd had a totally different—and surprising—reaction.

"Look, I'm sorry Tuck kicked you out, but I don't have a guest bedroom."

"I'll sleep on the couch. You won't even know I'm here." His face transformed from darkly sexual to a happy little boy's. "I don't have any other place to stay," he added, building his case. "You just said how grateful you are to Tuck for taking you in. I'm only asking for the same thing."

Damn, he had her. As much as she wanted to squash her feelings, some things did reach right under her shields. And some people . . . like Greer. Now, Darius's manipulation did. "All right," she spat out, feeling pinned.

Her phone rang from where she'd left it inside her truck.

"Thanks, Shea," Darius said, wheeling to his car and popping the trunk. "You're a doll."

She got into her truck, grabbing up the phone and eyeing the screen. Greer. She'd been trying to avoid him since moving out three months before. But with the weirdness going on lately, she needed to stay in the loop.

"Hey," she answered. "What's up?"

"Tuck and Darius had it out a while ago. Darius has this idea about being the alpha male, which is just stupid, and Tuck kicked him out. I wanted to let you know in case he shows up on your doorstep pulling his 'poor me' act."

"Too late," she said in a singsong voice. "Act pulled—very well, I might add. He's staying for a few days."

"Bad idea." Always the protective one. He made no apologies for it either.

She watched Darius lift his suitcase onto his lap and wheel toward the ramp he'd installed for wheelchair access to her front door. "Well, what was I supposed to do, turn him away? I don't like it either."

"I'm coming over."

"There's no need . . ." She looked at the screen, blinking to indicate he'd ended the call. ". . . to come over," she finished anyway.

She got out, feeling like her feet weighed fifty pounds each, and trudged to the door. All she wanted was to be alone, a quiet evening trimming her bonsai to clear her mind.

There would be no mind-clearing tonight. There'd be friction between Greer and Darius, just like there had been before she'd moved out. Tuck had eased her into the reality of Darkness, he and Greer morphing into black beasts only after she'd accepted the idea. Tuck told her it also made them fiercely, and insanely, territorial about their so-called mates. She hadn't thought twice about that until Darius and Greer both took a different kind of liking to her. She was afraid they'd tear each other's throats out, and she wasn't either of their mates.

"Two days," she said, unlocking her front door. "I like living on my own. Being alone." Most of the time. It was strange, but she'd sit at her table in the mornings having coffee (not as strong as Greer's k iller brew) and be happy about being alone. Then she'd get hit with a wave of sadness about being alone.

See how messed up you are.

"You might like having me around," he said. "If that guy

who's been creeping around makes an appearance, I'll kick his ass."

"Well, he's too much of a coward to knock on the door." She didn't want to think about her stalker. He hadn't left any of his icky letters or "gifts" in a few days.

She figured out where Darius could stash his suitcases and was hunting down extra sheets and a blanket when the doorbell rang. Before she could even set the extra pillow down to answer, she heard Darius's voice: "Well, look who's here. What a nice surprise."

Not by the tone in his voice. Damn, this was so not cool having them both here. They'd been like snarling dogs the day everyone had helped her move in here. She hadn't had them over since.

She walked out holding the pillow to her chest like a shield. Greer's eyes went right to her, giving her a clear *Is everything all right?* look.

She wasn't in danger. That's as far as she'd commit.

Greer closed the door and sauntered in, as though he always stopped by. "Thought I'd check in on you. After what happened, figured you might be on edge." There he went again, sinking her into the depths of his eyes. They were rimmed in gray, brown in the middle, the most unusual eyes she'd ever seen. And they were assessing her.

"She's fine," Darius answered as she opened her mouth. "I'm staying here for a couple of days, which will work out nicely . . . in case she's on edge." His unspoken *So you can go now* was clear.

Greer moved closer to her, putting himself physically between her and Darius. He was a damned wall of a man, too, way tall, wide shoulders, and just big. He purposely blocked Darius's view of her.

She'd done this, sparked them into hostile territory. Which was laughable, considering what she looked like: baggy pants and shirt, cap over her head, no makeup. She'd done everything she could for the last six years to squash every bit of her femininity. Her sexuality. Then Greer had blown that to bits.

He hadn't knocked, just barged into the bathroom, a towel loosely held in front of his naked body. She was drying her hair and suddenly he was standing there gaping at her.

"Jesus, Shea, you're beautiful," he'd said, obviously in shock.

She couldn't move, spellbound herself, which was ridiculous because she wasn't interested in anyone sexually. But there stood six feet four of olive-skinned Apache with muscled thighs and a scant bit of towel covering him. And the way he'd said those words, with his typical passion, and his looking at her like she *was* beautiful and he wanted her, woke up something inside her.

Breaking out of the spell and wrapping her towel around her, she'd yelled at him for barging in, stepping up close to him and jabbing her finger at his chest.

And what had he done? Lifted her damp hair from her shoulders, hair she never left loose, his fingers brushing her bare shoulders. "Why do you hide yourself from us?" he'd asked.

"Don't say anything about this to anyone." Would he tell them how oversized her breasts were? Would they wonder why she hid her curves, talking behind her back, speculating? "Leave. Now."

He'd shrugged, his dark brown eyebrows furrowing. "No

need to get mad or freaked out. It was an accident. We're friends."

He left, finally, and she looked in the steamy reflection. She didn't see beautiful. But she did see hunger, and even worse, felt it.

"How's your big job coming?" Greer asked now, pulling her out of the memory. He was leaning against the back of the couch, which inadvertently flexed the muscles in his arms.

He remembered, which touched her even if she didn't want to be touched. Still, she found herself smiling. "Great. We're putting the finishing touches now that the hard-scaping and most of the planting is finished. This is my biggest job yet. My business has kept me sane through all this. Gotta keep working on the customer's jobs." She glanced to the window. If the sun weren't going to be setting soon, she'd come up with some job she had to zip off to right then.

Dammit, she missed Greer. Hated having to shut him out. Now, things were odd between them. He looked at her differently, heat in his eyes, and hurt, too, because he didn't understand why she'd pushed him away. Like he'd said, it was an accident that he'd walked in on her.

"Do you want to stay for dinner?" she asked, not sure whether having them both there would be better than being alone with Darius.

Greer glanced at his watch. "Wish I could. My shift starts in an hour."

Darius wheeled up. "Yeah, the big bad firefighter, off to save lives." He made a superhero arm motion, pumping one fist in the air.

Greer's mouth twisted in a snarl. "I'd rather do that than tinker with computer parts all day."

"Boys," she said, sounding like a teacher.

Another knock on the door. Hopefully it was Tucker. He was good at stepping in. But it wasn't Tucker. Two men stood there, their badges at the ready. "Cheyenne Baker?" one of them asked.

She nodded, feeling Greer step up behind her.

"Detective Dan Marshall, and Detective Paul Marron. May we come in?"

"What's this about?" Greer asked before she could say anything.

"We have some questions about a recent incident." The man, in his forties, waited patiently for someone to invite them inside.

Greer inspected the badge, nodded to her. It was legit.

Shea checked it, too, then stepped back, bumping into Greer. "These are friends of mine," she said, waving to Greer and Darius.

Marshall closed the door behind them, taking in both men as though noting their appearance. He focused on her. "You've heard about the man who was mauled two nights ago?"

Her mouth went dry. How had they connected that to her? Bad enough that it triggered two men from the other dimension to hunt down their offspring. "Yes, it sounded horrible." She shuddered, and didn't have to fake it. "Wild animals attacking people in their own home."

"We don't think it was a wild animal. Do you know Fred Callahan, the victim?"

"No, I—" Her words jammed in her throat when she saw the picture he held up, a driver's license photo probably. All the blood drained from her face. "I knew him as Frankie C." She cleared the fuzz from her voice. "I haven't seen him for six years." She wanted the cops to go, or for Greer and Darius to leave. "I'm sorry, I can't help you."

Marshall's eyes flicked to Greer and Darius before returning to her. "We found pictures and notes about you on his computer. There was a letter in his desk drawer addressed to you, indicating he'd written to you before. It wasn't a very nice letter."

Her knees went weak. Greer somehow sensed it and clamped his hands on her shoulders. "What are you insinuating?" His hands started warming her, one of his psychic abilities.

Darius wheeled closer. "You can't possibly think this slip of a girl could tear a man apart."

"I've been getting letters, creepy gifts," she said. "But I didn't know who they were from." Frankie. She had wondered, yes, but how had he found her? And why after all these years?

"May I see them?" Marshall asked.

She'd wanted to throw them away, but thought they might be evidence if things escalated. She went to the file cabinet in her office and returned with the letters, and the box.

Marshall frowned when he opened it and saw the dildo, the flavored lube creams. "Can I take these?"

"Please." *And go. Say no more.*

He looked at Greer and Darius. "Did either of you know who was harassing her?"

Darius snorted. "No, but I'm glad the sick fu—the guy is dead. It's wrong to harass a woman like that."

Greer shook his head, but his gaze was on her.

Marshall turned to her again. "Callahan worked at the phone company. That's probably how he found you. You haven't heard from him at all in the six years since you filed charges against him and the other two men?"

"No, nothing," she said quickly. "I'd rather not—"

"I'm sure the detective you spoke to talked you out of going forward with the charges. I read the file and agree that it was a long shot to prosecute the case successfully. Still, I wish we had. One of those other men raped a teenaged girl a couple of years back. He's in prison now. The other's been jailed a few times on battery charges."

She felt Greer's questioning stare on her. "I'm sorry to hear that." Her words sounded shaky. *Leave, dammit.*

Marshall glanced in the box, then her. "But Callahan hasn't had another brush with the law. We did find some rather disturbing items in his home, including sex toys I presume he intended to send to you. One was a pair of handcuffs, and they weren't the fuzzy kind. It's the sort of thing that makes me uncomfortable about where he was going with this. So if you"—he looked at her friends—"or anyone had something to do with his death, it may have saved your life. But still, we have to investigate. It's a crime to tear a man apart, no matter how much of a scumbag he is."

"Son of a bitch," Greer said. His hands tightened on her as she slumped against the couch, and then he pulled her against his body, his arms like a shield over her collarbone.

Oh, God. Had Frankie been planning to rape her again? That overshadowed anything else in her mind at the moment.

Marshall seemed to be giving them time to fess up.

"We didn't know who the guy sending that stuff was," Shea said. "You can see from the letters that he never signed them." They'd been crude letters, detailing what he wanted to do to her body, and she'd forced herself to read them because she needed to know how much he knew about her. Or if they contained an explicit threat.

"Was it because of your earlier experience that you didn't report the stalking?" Marshall asked.

She shrugged, though it felt as though she wore an armored suit that smelled of a citrus cologne. "I didn't see it as threatening. Only gross and annoying."

Wrapped in Greer's embrace, she felt safe in a sea of chaos.

Marshall gave her his business card. "If there's anything else you know or remember, please give me a call." He took a step toward the door but turned back to her. "Ms. Baker, if anyone ever hurts you like that again, call me."

As soon as he left, Darius wheeled in front of her. "The guy's dead, Shea. You don't have to worry about him anymore. Isn't that great?"

Thank God Darius hadn't asked for more information. If only Greer would let it go.

He turned her to face him. "What happened? What was he talking about, if you're hurt 'again'?" His concern turned her to mush, and then his expression changed. He cradled her face, and as much as she wanted to push away, she couldn't. "Oh, Shea."

She heard it all in his voice—that he'd figured it out from

the detective's words. Raped "another" woman. She felt her expression crumple even though she tried to hold strong.

He pulled her against him, stroking her back. Her cap's brim bumped against him and it fell to the floor.

No, she had to push away. She would fall apart right here, and he would continue to hold her and soothe her, and it felt so good because no one had done that afterward. Not even her mother, who had the same opinion the cops did: that she deserved it.

She managed to move out of his embrace by reaching for her cap. She shoved it onto her head, pulling down the brim. "I'm fine. It was a long time ago."

"What are you two talking about?" Darius asked. At least he hadn't gotten it.

That was the difference between them, one of many. She wondered if Darius just had no emotions, nothing to squash or tuck away.

"You'd better go," she said to Greer, her voice thick. "You don't want to be late for your shift."

He was looking at her, probably giving her the same look he'd been giving her since the bathroom incident. The *Why are you shutting me out?* one. She couldn't tell, thankfully, because the brim of her cap blocked his eyes from view. At least he'd also pushed back after the bathroom incident and gone on, continued dating. He'd been cool to her afterward. That's what she wanted. Even if it stuck a knife in her chest.

"I do have to go. Walk me out." He took her hand, giving her no choice but to be dragged along with him.

The air was even more chilling now that the sun was setting. He paused by his Jeep, turning her to face him. "Shea, that's why you hide yourself, isn't it? Why you freaked when I accidentally saw you naked." He pulled off her cap. "Three of them?" His agony at the thought wracked his face.

"I don't want to discuss this. I freaked because I don't want people to see me naked."

"Because you've got curves—"

She pressed her hand over his mouth, feeling the full softness of it. "I am not interested in discussing my curves or my past."

"You're hurting, Shea. It's why you shut down on me. I lost a friend once, because he was hurting, too. Holding in a painful secret. I left for a while, doing construction out of town, and when I came back, he'd taken his life. He couldn't take the pain anymore."

"I'm not going to take my life. I've survived, gotten over it—"

"You haven't gotten over it." He tugged at her oversized shirt. "You hide your body. All those years you lived with us, you hid yourself. Did you think we'd hurt you? Attack you?"

He had no idea. "Of course not."

"That's why you were so pissed about me seeing you. Your secret was out."

That he had right. "That's ridiculous." She took the opportunity to look down at her attire, to escape those assessing eyes. "This is just how I like to dress."

He took his finger and lifted her chin. "I suddenly saw you as a woman and not just the girl who's lived with us for the past few years. Seeing you as a woman changed everything."

She smacked his arm, which probably hurt her more than him. "Then change it back. I don't want you like that."

He slowly blinked at her statement. "Is it because of what happened to you? We can work through that."

"Is he bothering you?" Darius called from the front step.

Greer muttered something very impolite under his breath, and then said, louder, "Go back in the house. We're talking."

Darius started to wheel down the ramp. "Whatever concerns Shea concerns me, too."

"I'm going in now," she said, dashing off before Darius could get close. As she suspected, he turned around and followed her back to the front step. Greer stayed by his vehicle, giving Darius a pissed look. She was glad Darius had stopped that conversation. Way too close for comfort on many levels.

"I'm fine, Greer," she called to him. "Thanks for caring. Get to work."

"Did I interrupt a tense moment?" Darius asked once he'd caught up to her, watching Greer's yellow Jeep back out. "Looked like he was harassing you. It had to do with whatever he did to you, didn't it? Tell me, and I'll make sure—"

"It's none of your business." She stalked into the house to find something for dinner, anything to get her mind off what just transpired.

It was hard to think about spaghetti or leftover steak when one question dominated her mind: how could it be a coincidence that the man who had been mauled was her rapist?